Let Love Have Its Way

BRE SMITH

authorHOUSE®

AuthorHouse™
1663 Liberty Drive, Suite 200
Bloomington, IN 47403
www.authorhouse.com
Phone: 1-800-839-8640

First published by AuthorHouse 10/21/2008

ISBN: 978-1-4389-1937-9 (sc)

Library of Congress Control Number: 2008909022

Printed in the United States of America
Bloomington, Indiana

This book is printed on acid-free paper.

Shout Outs

Friends…who yours are says much
about you. Choose wisely.
Proverbs 13:20

Don't you just hate it when you're all set to watch a great movie but before even the name of it floats across the screen, you've gotta be subjected to a gazillion credits and introductions – so and so presents so and so's production of a so and so film, and so it goes?

Well, I do too!

So if you're reading this page I realize you've probably already read the back cover, took another look at the front cover then flipped past the copyright page. Now here's another two pages full of acknowledgements.

I appreciate your indulgence. There are many, many people, who in the writing of this book pressed the pause button on the business of their own living to gently prod and strongly encourage me.

If I tried to list them all you would never get to the story. But there are a few who deserve to be called by name.

You don't have to guess who is at the top of the list.

Thank you God for never ever giving up on me. When I ignored your whispers you knocked me upside the head. When I was afraid you reminded me "I got this." When I finally found the courage to get out of my own way and let you take charge, you ordered my steps like a well written church bulletin. When I felt alone you brought forth a cast of loving friends and supporters. One by one they were there for me when I needed them most. Where I saw crisis and hopelessness you showed me opportunity and inspiration. By Your Grace I am who you chose me to be. Bless you Lord. I thank you and I praise you!

My children, Bridget, Conswella, Hunter and Alan, Jr. who love me for no other reason than I am their mother and stepmother.

Alan, Sr. who was my earliest and strongest supporter. Your challenging words years ago ignited the inspiration I needed to believe – "babes, anybody who can read four books at one time and keep up with all of them, can certainly write one of her own." Thank you Alan. I will forever be grateful for your love and support and for pushing me to see in myself what you saw in me.

My own **tiyospaye** - extended family. My 'other' Mom Cleatrice and the Johnson family, especially my best sister friend, Jen. The Archer family and Sylvia, Kathy and Tyra, thank you for your prayers.

Rita Starliper and Bill Snow – thank you for reminding me to listen to the whispers; That with love and friendship we can do whatever we want. I love you both.

Glennis Burton, who died way too soon. There will never be another like you Your inner strength and beauty were an inspiration to so many but none more than me. I love you for teaching me that among friends you don't need china and crystal when paper and plastic makes just as good an impression. I miss you Glennis.

Camilla Moore – you pushed so hard for me to keep climbing to the next level that sometimes I wanted to rip your hair out. But I learned two important lessons – always begin with the end in mind and write for the reader. I know now that if you hadn't loved me you would not have bothered. Thank you Cam.

Kate Bowers and Monique Tubbs – who loved me enough to suffer reading all the rewrites of my manuscript. All one millon of 'em!!! Now that's friendship. Thank you Girlfriends. Here's to the next martini.

Miss P. J. Robinson and PJ's Pen – a celebrity in her own right, whose editorial skills penned magic for a host of celebrities in every genre...from music to movies, from CNN to Hollywood, from philosophy to politics, from Theolonius Monk to Hilary Clinton. You made me feel just as important to you as any one of them. I appreciate your guidance and friendship.

My niece Angie – True Grit can't describe your persistence and determination. The life you created for yourself against overwhelming circumstances is a testament that God is still in the business of miracles. Your spirit of JOY, JOY, JOY after all you've been through is always an inspiration. You are beautiful, my niece. You never gave up on Auntie. I love you.

Nita- Girlfriend! Baby Sis! Life is just too damn short! Your unapologetic style of living life to the fullest and take no prisoners attitude puts you in a rare league of your own. I count myself blessed to call you my first and longest lasting sister friend.

Lisa Vallien Moore – how do I define your friendship? You took in a stranger, to your home, your heart and your family. When I said earlier that God put friends and supporters in my life when I needed them most, you were right there at the top. You saw my potential and force fed me until I acknowledged it. You listened, you empathized but you refused to let me get away with feeling sorry for myself. You have seen me at my worst yet you loved me more, not less. I am a better person because of you. I will forever treasure your friendship.

Carol Jackson – You taught me to keep it real. Aim high and never settle for less. Take the best life has to offer and don't apologize for being your best. Thank you Carol.

Pastor Joe Clavon – You didn't blink when you looked down at me from your pulpit and said "there is a book in you Bre. Write your book." Of course, after you read the first sentence in my book, you'll know it's not the one we had in mind. But don't fear Pastor Joe, it's on the way.

My brother Carl – You're a fool and I love you just as you are. Thank you for loving your sister, no matter what.

My niece LaShaune who doesn't judge, she just loves me. Thank you Niece.

Last but in no way least is DITTO. My debt to you is beyond any words I could write on this page. Your brutal honesty, your stubbornness, nagging, pushing, cajoling, admiration, encouragement, support and outright aggravation is a potent mix in my genie bottle. Each time I uncap it, you release whatever I need at the moment to keep me moving forward. Your message is simple "Work with what you got Bre." Now look what you've done. You made me a believer. I love you for that and am eternally grateful.

I am blessed to have many others in my life who lift me higher each day. I'm sorry I can't mention all of your names but you know who you are. Thank you. And to all of you who chose to buy and read this book, I am deeply grateful. I hope you are inspired by this story, whether it be to write your own or to commit to let love have its way in your life. I wish you Joy.

"I couldn't wait for success, so I
went ahead without it."

Jonathan Winters

Chapter 1

'Oh shit, Oh shit, Oh shit," Kizzie shouted loudly as she banged the steering wheel with both hands. Then, "oh shit" again as she felt the pain start in her left wrist, AGAIN. She had twisted it the day before when she was loading the Jeep. At the time she had been in too big a rush to stop and check out the damage, a lapse in judgment she now regretted.

Ignoring the fire snaking its way through every vein from wrist to elbow, Kizzie used that arm to maneuver the steering wheel while she double clutched, using the good right hand to shift from reverse to first. Almost in the same motion she gunned the gas pedal. The jeep lurched forward like it had been rammed with a bull dozer, taking off like the proverbial bat out of hell.

"Where in the Sam hill is that turn off?" Kizzie spoke out loud again.

Considered by family and all who knew her to have an excellent sense of direction and to be the best driver in nine counties, Kizzie was frustrated beyond belief to find her self in this predicament. She had looked forward to this day for many months, unlike any number of other events over the past year and a half that she would just as soon forget about.

She knew these roads like the back of her hand. Always had. Even though it had been seventeen years (with the exception of one visit five years ago that only lasted for twenty four hours but the whole town still talks about) since she had been in this town. But now, as then, not much about it had changed.

Now, having spent the last forty five minutes driving back and forth over the same five mile stretch of two lane asphalt was beyond her level of tolerance. To add to the frustration, Kizzie now realized she was going to be late.

She didn't have many pet-peeves; as a matter of fact she was normally quite calm about most things. The way she looked at it- Shit Happens! – move on! People are who they are, would do what they wanted to do and there was little, if anything, you could do to control the outcome.

Months ago, she had given up on the idea of trying to control anything outside of her own arm's reach. Her one exception to the pet-peeve thing was tardiness. On time for her was fifteen minutes early just for the ordinary day-to-day-get-up-get-dressed and get-to-work kind of day.

Special occasions, such as today, called for at least thirty minutes. Yet here she was, on a day she had looked forward to for months. And she couldn't find the damn turnoff for the road!

Well, obviously something had changed after all.

Kizzie had been on the road for the past three days. Normally she would have flown, first class, into the international airport at Rawlins, waited an hour for the connecting flight into the small, very small town of Clement, rented a car and drove the remaining hour to Smithville. But this trip would be different.

The original plan was to take the trip to her hometown for this so-called celebration and immediately turn around and fly home, as in the trip five years before. But as she was packing, she decided to do something totally out of character for her; something she had done only one other time in her life.

This time, she had a one way ticket via her Jeep and no plans beyond the next couple of days. This time, she had simply packed as many of her personal belongings as she could fit into her Jeep, emptied the contents of the refrigerator, had the power and phone disconnected, given her extra key to her townhouse to her neighbor, and left.

She left a message on her boss' answering machine with Cocoa's number, telling her that she could be reached there if, and only if, something came up that she absolutely had to talk to her about. She had no hotel reservations and no plans for what she was going to do with her life after this weekend.

Kizzie had not gotten a half mile down the road when something in her rear view mirror caught her attention. "Oh great." A cop. Or in this case, it would have to be the local Sheriff.

What else could possibly happen in one short twelve hour day?

As was her nature she quickly went through her options. She had been applauded as well as criticized many times for her ability to sum up any given situation, assess every angle, consider the options and make a decision, in the time it would take most folks to even get a grasp on what was going on.

In this case she figured she could choose one of two options. Stop or keep going. She was sure her Jeep could outrun any cop car this town put on the road. The one thing she didn't need was this local hick sheriff with a burr up his ass, who sure as hell had to think of himself as the town hero, holding her up for who knows how long, making her even later than she already was.

What was the worse that could happen if she kept going? He'd catch up to her in town and write her a ticket - for what she didn't even want to think about. But by then she could argue a case that he would have to prove whatever he wanted to charge her with. On the other hand if she stopped maybe he would just write the damn ticket for speeding and let her be on her way.

With that thought, she took another look in the mirror and almost laughed out loud. She didn't know what to make of what she saw. The sheriff's car was straight out of the Andy Griffith Show she loved to watch on TV. Up to and including the antennae. It curved from somewhere near the back bumper, over the driver side along the roofline and fastened to the front of the hood, making a wide arch. Black and white even!

What was different was the flashing light. Instead of just a clear light or even blue and white like most police vehicles anywhere, this one was purple and orange!

Kizzie's curiosity got the best of her. She had to know if the sheriff or whoever stepped out of that...thing...would be Barney or Andy. Then again she didn't think she wanted to know. Trying to hold off the laughter she took another look down at the speedometer and sucked in her breath. "Uh-OH."

Considering she had already slowed down by at least twenty miles per hour, she figured she had been clocked at about seventy! – in a forty five zone. "I don't think he's gonna be too happy," she mused as she slowed the Jeep until she came to a full stop on the graveled portion of the narrow road.

"Why the fuck did he stop me if he just plans to sit there like a jackass?" she wondered.

"Please give me a pass on that one Lord." She asked forgiveness for her curse word.

The arrow on Kizzie's patience meter was buried so deep in the left corner she actually thought about banging the steering wheel again. But with that snake still very much alive between her wrist and elbow, she let that idea die quickly.

She had been stopped for several minutes already and this knuckle head of a sheriff still hadn't moved from his car. She decided she wasn't waiting any longer.

She had the door open and her legs swung out and was just about to get out and ask him that very question when she saw him finally open his car door and start to approach her.

Chapter 2

The instant Zak got a full view of the legs, the butt and that skin the color of nicely browned toast who was Kizzie Carpenter; his outlook about the day took an instant 360 degree turn.

As Sheriff of this town, population one thousand if you counted the animals, part of his job and the part he disliked the most was to satisfy the council that he was cracking down on speeders along this stretch of Burning Cross Road.

A few years back an accident caused by speeding had been the cause of the town losing one of its leading citizens. Little did it matter that this had been the one and only serious accident even the oldest person in Smithville could remember.

The fine upstanding citizens who made up the town council were convinced that its accident rate was on the rise and would surely be the death of half the town. The council insisted that the Sheriff's office, namely Zak and his one lone deputy, "get out there and do something."

So Zak would, from time to time, "stake out" as Deputy Joe referred to it, here on this stretch five miles outside the town limits. At town meetings Zak would brief the council on the success of his "cracking down".

So far in two years the "stake outs" had netted exactly ten tickets, mostly to out-of-towners, since most of the locals always knew exactly where Zak would be cracking down on any given day.

It seems his Deputy Joe liked to boast a little too much about the fine tuned operations of the Sheriff's department and after having one too many beers at Stoney's on his days off would invariably tell anyone within earshot just where the next "stake out" operation would take place.

Truth be told, Zak would spend all of about an hour in this grove of trees just off the interstate. Even at that he was usually bored out of his senses so he'd play solitaire. The deck he shuffled now had been worn thin from use.

He much preferred to shut the whole operation down and pay a visit to Seal's, his on again, off most of the time, girlfriend who lived a few miles from the stake out. Well, not exactly girlfriend. He'd only been with her once; a moment of weakness when he first got back into town ten years ago.

Even before the date was over, she'd already started in on him about'when are you going to find Kizzie, are you going to tell her, and on and on.'

He actually hadn't been to her place in months. He didn't need the headache. There was no lack of venom being spit at him every time he came within breathing room of her in town.

Thinking better about it Zak decided he would rather take on one of the errands for the townsfolk. His 'operation' consisted of pulling over the first out-of-towner who was unlucky enough to veer off the interstate in search of the fine home cooking at Miss Eddie's diner which was advertised, along with her picture, on three billboards one mile apart just before the exit. And if they weren't exactly hungry, their curiosity about Miss Eddie would surely get the best of them.

Some years back Miss Eddie had been convinced, everyone thought, by a visiting artist that he could paint her beautiful on canvas. The artist, being more talk than talent, unfortunately painted Miss Eddie in the most hideous colors one could imagine.

You see Miss Eddie, all 309 pounds was 'beauty challenged' as the nicer women of the church's Lady Auxiliary would call her; but was more accurately described by her best friend.

It had been reported once that Miss Frances, best friend to Miss Eddie, had been known to inform her friend that it was fortunate for her daughter that she took after her father because her mother was just pure dee ugly.

It was because Miss Frances was no raving beauty herself, Miss Eddie forgave her for that remark so she lived to see another birthday after saying so. Anyone else would not have been so fortunate.

Miss Eddie, seventy five if she was a day, was indeed a large woman. She carried her 309 pound, six foot frame inside a cover of dark chocolate skin that was, winter or summer, spring or fall, white with ash.

Lacking teeth, and refusing to wear dentures, her cheeks were sunken as though she had sucked them in to make a smacking kiss and forgot to let the air out again. The wrinkles started just below the hairline on her forehead and worked their way down in folds until they faded into the rolls of her chin.

But Miss Eddie had two of the finest redeeming features you would ever want to see – her hair, worn normally in a plait that fell to her hip bones- was snow white from age; the other, big beautiful brown eyes that never seemed to age, twinkled with the smile missing from her mouth.

The artist had convinced her that her portrait would be that much more beautiful if she unplaited her hair and let it fall loose around her shoulders which she indeed chose to do.

The day the portrait was revealed was an event the people of Smithville were still talking (and laughing) about; though no one dared laugh while Miss Eddie was looking.

Miss Eddie, being pleased and proud of her portrait, had persuaded Miss Frances to 'present' it at the end of one particular Woman's Day service after church. The portrait was present. Miss Eddie wasn't.

Now, on most Sundays, the minister could count on having maybe fifty people total, for both the early and afternoon services. It was rumored that Miss Eddie served up more than 'fine food' at her restaurant, and her menu catered mostly to the menfolk in town. And of course those out of towners.

When word got out that Miss Frances intended to 'present' Miss Eddie's portrait, there wasn't an empty seat to be found. It seemed the whole town had shown up to be among the first to see how the artist had brought out the best of Miss Eddie's fine features.

When Miss Frances removed the cloth that had kept the artist's subject hidden, the entire congregation leaned forward in their pews as if they were a single body. You could literally hear a pin drop.

Then one after the other the murmurs started.

"Oh my!

"Mercy's sakes!"

"My goodness!

"Where'd she find enough cloth? Who made the dress?"

" How'd she get up on that bar?"

It took only a few minutes for the initial shock to sink in. Then the snickering began; first in the front pews closest to the portrait. By the time the snickers reached the last row, they had turned into outright laughter.

They weren't exactly laughing at Miss Eddie. If you could get past the hideous colors the artist had chosen for her dress, the portrait wasn't that bad.

There she was, stretched out on top of the bar in her diner. She was supporting herself with her right arm underneath her. It held a huge red rose against her stomach. Her left was raised and folded across her head, palm out. Her right leg was flat against the bar top and bent in at the knee. Her left crossed over the right and was propped in the air, her toes pointing upward. She wore no shoes.

The mountain of material that was her dress had a pheasant top pulled low off the shoulder. The jewel neck was cut so deep it showed cleavage deep enough to swim in. Her hair fell loose around the flesh of her large arms inside the sleeveless top, hiding some of the folds of flesh around her neck.

The bottom of the dress was draped across the knee of the leg propped in the air. It was tucked in slightly at the vee where her thighs met. The rest fell over her right leg and off the side of the bar. The artist had painted the huge thighs, calves and ankles so that the flesh appeared firm and tight. At the bottom of the portrait the artist had painted, Serving the 'finest food' in the county.

What was funny was that it was almost sexy! And Miss Eddie's audacity to do such a thing at her age then to take it one step further and reveal it in church, took nerves most of them wished they had.

They didn't know it but there was a reason for Miss Eddie's self defiance at this stage of her life. They would all know soon enough what it was.

Chapter 3

Zak was forty four, six four with skin the color of a ripe pecan. Body tight and muscular and would hold up against any twenty five year old in town. He had a head full of black tiny curls so thick and soft that Seal and any other woman of legal age spent as much time as they could, trying to think of a reason to get Zak to let them run their fingers through it- that is again, if you paid attention to what the good towns people had to say about it.

Most of the time he kept his hair in braids; this as a compromise with the town council who wanted him to wear the standard military crew cut that they thought portrayed the proper dignity of his position as the Sheriff. The council had made this proposal when they made him the job offer and without hesitation, Zak had refused hands down.

When he wasn't busy being Sheriff - and in a town the size of this one that could be anywhere from an hour to several hours during the day - he spent much of that time helping some of the older citizens as the local handyman.

He could be found at Miss Eddie's banging boards back into place on a porch he was convinced was unsafe for the average person to step on, to say nothing of Miss Eddie at her weight. But she refused to let him tear it down and build another one.

Or over at Miss Gertie's chopping and stacking firewood for the beautiful and original cookstove with reservoir that she cleaned and polished as though it were a piece of the finest furniture; and still used to cook every meal even with the brand new GE sitting right next to it.

Mr. Tanner, the town's oldest citizen, stooped from age and requiring the use of a cane, was still almost as tall as Zak, needed help with keeping the grass cut. Well, he didn't exactly NEED help. He was as healthy as a horse and twice as strong. Cutting the grass would have been easy for Pa Tanner- he had simply quit cutting it when Mrs. Tanner had called him out of his name the last time he had cut it and somehow managed to run over one of her newly planted bed of mums.

Zak had been just about ready to pull up stakes and go find out what chores awaited him today when he had first noticed the Jeep make more that one trip in the past half hour past where he was shadowed in the grove of trees.

He decided to investigate after he checked his radar that showed a speed that any sane person would be crazy to be going, local or out of towner. It was after he had reached up to turn on his flashing lights that it occurred to him exactly who this was.

He would bet his life on it!

He decided to have some fun.

Chapter 4

"Was there a reason you stopped me Sher...." Kizzie almost choked when she realized who she was looking at when he stuck his face up to her open window. But being Kizzie, she quickly recovered and finished her question as though nothing at all had happened to her insides. "Sheriff?"

This after what seemed liked forever to Kizzie since Zak had taken his time to mosey up to her Jeep then was just standing there gawking at her like she had horns on her head.

She recognized him instantly, even after all these years, but she refused to give him the personal greeting she was sure he expected that would validate that recognition. She simply said again, "Well, Sheriff" this time heavy on the sarcasm with the title instead of using his name.

He grinned. Her heart melted! She hated him! He was in love just as he had been all his life!

For his part Zak was amused and not in the least put out with her sarcastic slight. "Kizzie Carpenter-well I'll be damned". Love of my life and just as beautiful as ever. How the hell are you?"

Kizzie was not amused. "Tired as a dog, way behind schedule and in about another thirty seconds if you don't get on with this 'sheriff' business, I'm about to be really pissed off. So you wanna tell me why you stopped me."

"Whoa darlin'-why the hate" I'm just trying to tell you how great it is to see you. But we'll get back to that later on this evening. Right now, this 'sheriff', using her tone, would really like to know how come you just flew past me back there like a haint is after you. Precious."

Kizzie didn't know what to respond to first...the darlin', getting back to this later this evening', the haint comment or the 'Precious'.

She did know she was getting more agitated by the second so she let all that pass for now, growling "like I said I am way behind schedule. And what's the big deal about going a little over the speed limit anyway. It's not like this road is exactly busting with traffic."

All this she said without turning her head to look at him. One thing she didn't let pass. Turning her head oh so slowly and with eyes of fire she gave him the look he knew was coming -"And don't fucking call me Precious".

"OK I'm two for two Lord," went through her mind as soon as the words left her lips.

Zak, still in no hurry at all, crossed his arms and leaned forward into the open window of the Jeep until his lips were just inches away from that pretty brown cheek he had been crazy about since he was eight years old.

…"seventy in a forty five Precious?" I wouldn't exactly call that a 'little' over the speed limit." He again used the pet name he had adopted for her the very first time he had seen her all those years ago and knew she would remember, and be pissed!

Kizzie felt his breath on her cheek. A thousand memories from her childhood rushed her like a brain freeze when she bit into too much ice cream.

She attempted to brush his face aside with the same left wrist she had banged the steering wheel with earlier. Wrong! Zak kept talking. "If I didn't know better, I'd swear you were kind of anxious to get to that little shindig being held in your honor tonight…"

"What shindig? What are you talking about and what do you have to do with it?"

Same old Kizzie. Zak knew there was nothing she hated more than surprises and could never ever stand to be teased. He was guessing that right about now if she had a gun he would be one dead Sheriff.

He had pulled his head away from the window just in time to miss the swipe she threw at him. Now he stuck it back in and in his best Forest Gump imitation said "and that's all I got to say about that".

In the space of less than ten minutes Kizzie had gone from having her heart thump out of her chest, to hating him, heart melting, hating him again and now back to remembering why she had loved him all her life. He could always, always make her laugh.

But this time she was in no mood. She'd be damned if she would let him see the smile making a steady march from her heart to her face. "Clifford Zacharias Bishop-just give me the damn ticket or whatever you're gonna do and let me get on my way.".

"Now see that sounds like you're trying to open up negotiations..."

Before he could finish, Kizzie moaned "Oh God. Here we go". She knew what was next.

Zak continued as though he hadn't heard. "Seeing as how if I was to write out that ticket, I'd have to run your drivers license; that could take about ten, fifteen minutes. Then to get everything written down for the record, well...(this he drew out like notes in a song) that could be another five or ten. Might be awhile before you reached town. Besides, seventy in a forty five, that could get expensive."

Those childhood memories again!

When they were kids this practice of negotiating had been born purely as a figment of Zak's imagination and he used it whenever he felt he had the advantage to get what he wanted...mostly kisses from her.

Anytime she had needed him, even for the smallest thing, and more of the times she didn't, he would charge her a 'toll'. From fixing her bike, to talking his friends into letting her tag along with them, to covering for her when she got in trouble with grown-ups, it didn't matter.

And he would always start out with... "Well now, it sounds like we might have to negotiate..."

"But I didn't ask you to open that door for me. I could've done it for myself."

"What?" You know Miss Lizzie would want me to be a gentleman."

"Don't even mention my mother. Besides, I don't think she would call anybody who used blackmail to get what he wants a gentleman."

Of course he denied it. They would go back and forth until it got on Kizzie's nerves.

She would hold out, sometimes for hours, but would end up giving in just to get it over with.

Back then, after her very reluctant, "OK, fine" he would ever so slowly lean down and plant the sweetest kiss on one cheek then do the same to the other.

She would wait very patiently while he did so and then haul off and hit him in whatever area was closest to her at the time and politely stomp off.

He would watch her walk off while he tried to figure out how to stop his heart from jumping out of his chest.

This time the memory was causing her to be more pissed than ever. "Why don't you just grow up?" But she knew that once he had his mind made up, he would be as stubborn as she and they could be sitting out here for the next hour.

As she muttered "Whatever..." she turned her head again to face the window. He had leaned in closer and no sooner than she turned she met his lips head on. He was estatic! She was livid!

Without another word she once again used that left hand to maneuver the wheel and the right to jam into first gear. In her rear view mirror she saw Zak dancing around trying to avoid being hit by flying gravel.

Already at seventy by the time she hit third, she was not sorry.

Looking after her, he mumbled "Oh Precious... there is a God." He made no pretense about how happy he was. "let me do my happy dance."

Chapter 5

Kizzie finally rolled into the edge of town. She checked her watch. Almost five o'clock. Even though the sun was still high in the sky and there was still plenty of daylight; Kizzie felt like it should have been midnight. And her day was just beginning.

"What the…"

Kizzie was absolutely floored!

When she had finally gotten past Miss Eddie's diner, the episode with Zak, still flying like a bat out of hell, and rounded the last corner which put her directly in front of town square, she had stopped the Jeep on a dime right where she was, in the middle of the street. Another foot further and she would have run right through the barricade that had been set up to close down Main Street.

The huge banner, which had to be twenty five feet deep, strung high above the street from one side to the other, was the first thing to grab her attention. Letters, equally as large and painted on in bright fluorescent colors that would no doubt glow even at the darkest of midnight, proclaimed 'Welcome Home Kizzie' on the top line and 'Our Shero' just below.

Kizzie didn't know if it was on purpose that the letter H had been usurped with a huge S in front of it or if some local kids had thought it an adventure to talk Dicey down at the fire department into hoisting one of them up on his ladder truck to change it.

However it came to be, there was no doubt this was for her and the beginnings of the 'shindig' Zak eluded to earlier.

She had little time to think about it as she realized, as if coming out of a deep sleep, that both sides of the wide street were lined with more people than she could count. There must be people there not only from her little town but from miles around.

Every single one of them had a handful of huge colorful balloons, thousands of balloons. Children sitting high atop their parents' shoulders, swinging from tree limbs and standing on tops of buildings waved flags and banners.

Then she heard the noise. They were clapping, yelling, blowing party horns, whistles and any other noise maker they could get their hands on.

As sure as she knew this was all for her, Kizzie knew who was responsible. And she was going to choke the living shit out of her as soon as she could lay hands on her.

And if she knew her friend Cocoa, this was a scary prelude to all the evening would offer.

She had known that she would be required to make the customary appearance; she had thought, no - she had hoped, it would be no more than maybe a dinner with the council members and a few guests, perhaps in the church basement or the school auditorium.

She would let them ooohhh and aaaahhh. She would make the appropriate 'thank yous', shake a few hands, then ease her way to the cozy little room at Cocoa's, already made up and waiting for her and fall blissfully asleep.

That obviously was not the plan. When Cocoa had told her it would be "just a 'little' something in your honor" she should've guessed that 'little' was not the right term to describe anything her friend set her mind to do...but this, this was absurd!

The eyes were watching her, expecting her to do something. She still couldn't move.

Kizzie tried to shake herself from the frozen state she seemed to have gone into trying to take this all in. It was too much all at once.

She made herself focus on the scene in front of her. Since she couldn't move a muscle, she let her eyes absorb one bit at a time as though she were putting together a puzzle.

Ahead and to her left was Cocoa. Knowing Cocoa she would have fought tooth and nail to make sure she was in the right position to be the first one her friend would see. At forty she still looked as she had since they were teens – drop dead gorgeous.

As usual she was standing on at least three inch hi heeled sandals. Her long, perfectly shaped brown sugar legs, seemed to go on forever, ending in a pair or white hip hugger shorts that stopped just about mid thigh.

Standing five ten on flat feet her legs needed no help from hi heels but for as long as she had known her, Kizzie had never seen Cocoa wear anything less than three inches high.

The shorts were set off with a belt drawn through large loops and crowded with silver studs that perfectly matched the studs across the toes of her sandals.

Her top was a tie dyed sleeveless waist shirt which covered a black tube top over perfectly round grapefruit sized breasts and tied at a perfectly sized twenty eight hourglass waist.

Her skin was flawless, as it had been all her life. It was the color of light brown sugar in the winter and dark brown sugar with a summer tan.

Her perfectly shaped almond eyes were the color of liquid amber and a mouth full of gleaming white teeth.

But as stunning as that combination was, the most extraordinary thing about Cocoa was her beautiful, long, snow white hair that she always, always wore in a perfectly shaped ponytail.

Unlike Miss Eddie's that had turned white with age, Cocoa had been born with this mop and no amount of peroxide had worked to change it. Even though most of the people here had grown up with her; some who had teased her unmercifully causing her to learn how to fight, most of them still did a double take whenever they saw her.

Still, as beautiful as she was on the outside, it was nothing compared to the beauty of her warm spirit. Even though they had seen each other only on rare occasions over the past seventeen years, they were the rarest of best friends. No matter what the event, when they were together it was as though time had stood still.

As much as Kizzie hated all the fuss and bother of this whole charade, she took one look at her dearest friend's beaming smile and knew she was home. For a moment she forgot all about how good it would feel to have her hands wrapped around that perfect little throat.

She let her eyes continue to piece together the scene. Next to Cocoa stood Cocoa's cousin Seal and her two brothers.

Her eyes locked with Seal's in a cold stare that lasted several seconds until Seal finally broke the contact and looked away.

In back of them were all the members of the council; Mr. Grady who owned the one and only bank, Mr. Young, the grocery store, Miss Gertie who owned the cleaners, Miss Suzie, the beauty parlor, Mr. Bloom the department store owner and Jesse White, the gas station.

Then there were the Adkins twins, Solomon and Burke, who were in her class the year she graduated high school. They were a year older than her but she had been allowed to skip seventh grade. Miss Eddie, who you couldn't miss, had closed her diner and was here for the occasion.

They must really have some shindig planned, thought Kizzie. She couldn't remember a time when Miss Eddie's diner had been closed during the day, especially on a weekend.

Her eyes continued to glance over the crowd. They were all there. She tried to match the other faces with memories from her childhood but found it almost impossible to do. There were just too many and too much time had passed for her brain to shuffle all those names around at the moment to match them with a face.

Just off to the right and behind Cocoa was Cocoa's mother and step father. Her own mother and father had died together when she was still a teenager. Cocoa's family had taken her in and treated her just like one of their own.

It was no surprise to see them here today, beaming almost as much as Cocoa.

Chapter 6

Kizzie knew she had to make a move instead of just sitting here like an idiot caught in a time warp.

It seemed like she had been sitting there for hours but knew it had only been a few minutes.

She was suddenly conscious of the nagging pain still in her left wrist, the hum of the jeep's motor she hadn't bothered to turn off and her right foot pressing down so hard on the brake her leg was actually trembling from the strain. The jeep was still in gear and her left foot still on the clutch.

"This is not real."

One more glance out her windshield made that thought a negative. The crowd was still banging the noise makers and everyone was still waving and smiling.

Shaking her head quickly from side to side and taking a deep breath, she killed the jeep's engine and ever so slowly opened the door and stepped down.

"Here she comes, here she comes." Kizzie couldn't make out where the chant was coming from but the crowd, as if waiting for it as a signal, suddenly went dead silent.

It lasted for as long as it took her to make her way around to the front of the jeep. No one moved.

As she walked around the barricade, Cocoa was the first to move, then they were around her all at once; Cocoa's parents, the twins, Seal and her brothers, all trying to touch her and hug her at the same time.

She felt Cocoa's mother's arms around her from one side and Cocoa on the other.

"My rocks." She hugged back.

"Move, you people. Let the girl get some air. You gon' smother her to death." This from a loud megaphone set up on a podium further into the center of town that Kizzie had failed to even notice.

"Get out the way now and let the girl come up here so's we can give her a proper welcome.

"Joe Clark," the voice called. "Joe Clark! DEPUTY!! The voice yelled, getting louder each time. "Get them people to the side so Miss Carpenter can have some room to walk."

Kizzie noticed the deputy for the first time. She didn't know him. He wasn't very tall, not more than about five six, but stocky. He wore a uniform similar to the one she had seen on Zak earlier; light tan khaki pants with a dark stripe down the outside of each leg and matching shirt with short sleeves for the summer.

The collar to his shirt was open, revealing a patch of tight small round hair at the edge of his undershirt.

He was what Cocoa would call light-skinned with short cropped hair that looked like it was just how the Council would want it. Brown eyes and a wide mouth. He wore a thin mustache and a short goatee, which he obviously spent a lot of time on. It was trimmed to a tee.

As if realizing he was indeed in charge of crowd control, Deputy Joe sprung into action. He began working his way through the center of the crowd, motioning people on either side of him to step back.

"OK people, OK people, you heard the Mayor. Let's make room for the little lady to come through."

"Little lady?" She had him in age by at least ten years. Kizzie remained quiet but let herself be moved along with the motion of the crowd, still Cocoa on one side; the parents and twins on the other.

As they got closer to the podium, the Mayor continued to offer encouragement, as if she needed to be coached along.

"That's right, that's right, you just come right on up here by me now so these folks can get a real look at 'ya."

"Does everybody in town repeat each word twice," Kizzie whispered in Cocoa's ear, although she couldn't figure out why she was whispering, with all the racket going on.

"Cocoa, I swear to God"...Kizzie threatened, under her breath with a frozen grin on her face.

"You can thank me later," her friend said as she took her by the hand and hauled her up the remaining steps to the platform where the podium and the Mayor were waiting.

Handing her off to the Mayor, who Kizzie recognized now as Mr. Dennis, "Dicey", as everyone called him – the fire chief down at the firehouse, if you could seriously call it that.

The last time she had been home there was one fire truck and all of three volunteers on the fire squad who could be found most days anywhere but at the firehouse. Except for Dicey, who took his job just as seriously as Deputy Joe.

Dicey had convinced the town many years back that if the town ever had a real fire, half the town would burn because there was no decent fire truck. The council had relented and purchased the ladder truck and Dicey had become a different man.

Mayor Dennis was speaking into the megaphone trying to get the crowd to quiet down. Apparently he had prepared a speech for this occasion and was determined for everyone to hear it.

Kizzie still felt as though she was in a fog. She didn't know if it was from being tired combined with the lack of sleep or if she was in shock at the unexpected celebration.

She had talked on the phone with Cocoa any number of times during the past several months. She never once uttered a word!

That in itself was amazing to Kizzie since Cocoa normally couldn't wait to spill the details about anything that went on in this town. She never kept secrets from Kizzie but anyone else couldn't pry her lips open with a crow bar if she chose to keep it to herself.

"If I could have your attention please," the Mayor was saying, in a tone that made it all too apparent that this was not the first time he'd said it.

Kizzie looked out at the sea of faces in front of her. There was not an inch of standing room left in the whole town square.

As waving flags became still, noise makers grew silent and the loud voices became murmurs, Kizzie could see the eyes of those closest to the stage glance first to the Mayor and then settle on her.

She somehow knew, even though she couldn't see them, that all the others did the same.

Now that the Mayor believed he finally had their full attention, he continued. "I won't take a lot of your time today folks – I'll do that on Monday at the dedication".

There were chuckles that rumbled though the crowd. It seems the Mayor was known for sometimes being long winded.

"I don't have to tell you all what a special day this is for Smithville. One we have waited a long time to see. I also don't have to tell you that it is all because of this young lady standing up here beside me. So even though you all have been having a great time today, right?"

There was more applause, flag waving and shouting that went on another full two minutes before the Mayor was allowed to continue.

…"we can't forget the reason we're here and that this day is in her honor." With that he turned to face Kizzie.

"Miss Carpenter. Kizzie. We know you've come a long way to be with us today. You'll have to forgive us for pouncing on you the minute you got into town and dragging you up here, putting you on display like Miss Eddie's portrait."

There were more snickers from the crowd.

"Were it not for you, this town would have been erased from the map. We are sincerely hoping that over the next couple of days we'll be able to show you our gratitude. And how very, very pleased we are that you accepted our invitation to come today. But...we know you're tired and probably anxious to get away from all these knuckle heads..."

"Who you calling knuckle head Mayor?"

"...and we'll let you get to that in a few minutes. First, as Mayor and on behalf of everyone you see here and hundreds more you don't, we want to extend you a very warm welcome and to tell you Welcome Home, Miss Carpenter."

The crowd went wild again. Kizzie returned the firm handshake and smiled as a camera from somewhere she couldn't see snapped several pictures of her and the Mayor.

"Now folks, he directed back to the crowd again, "I know you all want to shake her hand and say hello yourselves. There'll be plenty of time for that over the next couple days. Right now I want you all to make way for her and let her go on and get settled over at Miss Mazie's."

Kizzie mumbled a quick 'thank you' amid the loud applause as she made her way down from the platform.

She thought to herself " it seems everybody knows my itinerary except me." Cocoa was waiting at the bottom step and reached out to grab her hand. She soon had to let go in order for Kizzie to shake the hands outstretched to her. Her right arm was in as much pain from the handshakes as her left by the time they made their way back through the throngs of people to her Jeep.

She never noticed that Zak had watched the entire proceedings from his perch at the back of the crowd. He'd used his police binoculars and had never taken his eyes off of her.

Once back at the Jeep, Kizzie sat down on the front bumper. Cocoa did the same.

""I am truly speechless. I have no idea what to say, except I see Cocoa Sullivan written all over this little 'shindig'.

"Shindig?"

"Yeah, that's what our friend, Mr. Clifford Zacharias Bishop informed me of earlier."

"Zak? You've seen Zak already?"

Kizzie told her about meeting up with Zak earlier.

"Well, I'll bet that's one happy S.O.B."

"Did you hear what I just said? I cussed the man out, who happens to be the Sheriff, and showered him with gravel and dust. Why exactly would that make him happy?"

"Because he happens to worship the ground you walk on, that's why. He always has."

"Zak hasn't seen me in seventeen years."

"Eighteen but who's counting. And so what does time have to do with anything? That still doesn't stop him from asking me every single time I see him for your phone number...did you give her my number – Yessss! Did she say she was gonna call me?..Noooo. I finally told him, Zak, if she wants you to know where she is, she'll call you."

"How in the world did he get to be the Sheriff?"

"He'll have to fill in the details for you himself but about five years ago, soon after your last visit, Sheriff Skinner's wife forced him to retire. She literally gave him thirty days to do it. I guess he'd promised her more than once that he would but claimed he couldn't find any jerk in this town with enough brains to handle the job.

Well, this time she made it clear that he'd better find somebody and he'd better do it fast. Next thing anybody knew, Zak's name got thrown in the ring, the council votes unanimously (which has never happened as far as any of us can remember) for him, made him an offer and a month later, he was being sworn in."

"But Cocoa, it's Zak. Our Zak. The one we grew up with. The one who was in so much trouble all the time he should've had his name changed. He got into fights, got drunk, speeding tickets, disorderly conduct. You name it. Zak broke every rule and every law on the book and then created his own just to have more to break. How on earth does somebody like that enforce the laws he's been hell bent on breaking his whole life?"

"Don't ask me, honey child. But he's a great Sheriff. Everybody says so. But look at Dicey. Whoever would have thought he'd be the fire chief!"

Anyway, here comes Ma. You know she's got a mountain of food waiting for you and there's no way you're gonna convince her you're not hungry."

The crowd was breaking up and everyone going their own way; some in groups, others in couples and some lone souls lumbering off by themselves.

One thing was sure; it was Friday night and that meant that wherever they ended up, the parties would continue.

But party was the last thing on Kizzie's mind. Right now, she actually was hungry and would love to crunch down on some of Miss Mazie's fried chicken. After that all she wanted was to soak for hours in a nice hot bath. A couple of strong aspirin for her wrist would be good too.

"Hey girl, nice Jeep. Very nice. I'm riding with you. Wow! What's with all the stuff!"

"Long story. Tell you later," Kizzie said just before she hit the clutch.

Cocoa wasn't the least concerned that she had left her newly restored, classic and beautiful Mercedes parked, and unlocked, right in front of Miss Suzie's Beauty Salon.

After finally weaving her Jeep through the chaos down at the Square, Kizzie listened as Cocoa started in on the details, filling her in on the latest gossip.

Cocoa never took part in the creation of any gossip but she made sure to absorb every word so she could relay it all to Kizzie whenever she would hear from her.

The one sided conversation had continued right through the dinner of fried chicken, potatoe salad and tons of fresh home grown vegetables. Kizzie begged off from dessert, only by promising to have a double portion at Sunday's dinner.

Cocoa did no such thing.

Kizzie was grateful that Cocoa's family didn't push her to spend a lot of time with them that evening. She didn't think she could take another second of excitement today.

Kizzie started to shed her clothes as soon as she hit the front door at Cocoa's then headed straight for the bathroom.

She knew her way.

After an hour she peeled herself from under the ton of bubbles and water that had gone from steamy hot to barely luke warm. She had literally fallen asleep in the tub.

Chapter 7

In spite of all the promises she had made to herself and swearing up and down that she would not be drawn in by his charms, Kizzie was doubled over on the couch, arms scissored across her waist holding her sides, laughing so hard tears streamed down her face; she was just about two laughs away from literally peeing her pants.

She could not remember the last time she had laughed so hard. At one time she had loved to laugh but over the past few years if she had smiled at all, it seemed perfunctionary and was short lived.

One of the things about Zak was that he never failed to make her laugh. The down in the gut, tears streaming, soul cleansing kind of laugh that left you feeling warm and wonderful for a long time afterward.

This particular episode had started during a game of bid whist. Cocoa and her current boyfriend Thomas (though Cocoa would put a stake in anyone's heart, including Kizzi's if they called him that to her face) Zak, and she had been in the midst of heated up-towns, low bids, reneging and loud talking, helped along by some high octane drinks served up by Cocoa, when Zak got started on one of his stories.

Earlier that evening, Thomas, claiming to have stopped by to drop off 'a little money' he had promised Cocoa, but really just hoping to get lucky and get laid, had been the first to interrupt Kizzie and Cocoa's girl session that had started in the Jeep and continued as soon as Kizzie had emerged from the bathroom, curling herself into Cocoa's delightful couch.

Kizzie had asked Cocoa again to explain to her just why in hell she had put the whole town up to such a stunt.

Cocoa, thinking Kizzie quite ungrateful, had given her the same answer as the last ten times she'd asked. "Why the fuck not? You made it happen didn't you? Stop bitching about it and enjoy the fun."

"You're such a lady." Kizzie threw back.

"No call, no notice, just shows up and walks in like he owns the place."

It took a moment for Kizzie to realize that Cocoa was not talking to her but at this giant walking in through the open back door from the porch.

He was taller than Cocoa by more than a couple inches with a basketball player's physique; large muscular arms and thighs but skinny legs below the cut off jeans he wore with a tee shirt that fit tightly across his chest.

Cocoa had heard about Thomas, one of many men Cocoa seemed to have on a short leash at any given time, ready to do her bidding.

Cocoa had told her that Thomas was so ugly she had warned him to never show up at her house in the daylight. She said he was too ugly to be seen by her neighbors and he'd better not ever be caught there by any of her friends.

Thomas would ignore any such warning, in spite of having been told those exact words to his face, and come creeping whenever he felt like it only to suffer a royal ass kicking via Cocoa's mouth.

This time, probably for Kizzie's sake, Cocoa didn't say another word – just stared at Thomas for a few seconds more, then headed back to her place on the couch.

Before she could sit back down, another visitor. This time it was Zak. Kizzie had stopped in the middle of whatever she was about to say.

Following her gaze, Cocoa forgot Thomas for the moment and turned her attention toward whatever was distracting Kizzie.

Zak had changed from the police uniform and was now decked out in black jeans that looked like they were tailor made for his body – no room to spare but not too tight either.

He wore a white shirt with thin black pin stripes, open three buttons down from the collar and tucked in neatly at the waist. No belt and had slipped his feet into open toed sandals closed in at the heel, two Velcro strips were in place across the tops.

The cap he'd worn earlier was gone and so were the braids. All this Kizzie had taken in in an instant. She couldn't help but marvel that for his age, Zak Bishop was still a very, very handsome creature.

Thinking about how sloppy she was dressed made her wish she could dissolve right into the chair cushions. She was more than a little disturbed that she even cared. It was just Zak.

Cocoa couldn't hold it back this time. "Don't any of you people know whose house this is! That door is there for a reason." It wasn't a question. " Stop walking the hell up in my house like you pay the damn mortgage."

Zak, unfazed as usual, looked over at Thomas, who he apparently knew and knew very well if the look of mischief that passed between them was any indication.

"What she trying to say, man. You see any door. I don't see no door. If I'd a seen any door, I would've knocked on it. Trying to say our Mamas didn't teach us no manners."

From his tone you would have thought his feelings were terribly hurt.

Kizzie and Cocoa knew better. Zak kept on walking until he reached the couch and plopped down in the space beside Kizzie that Cocoa had vacated earlier.

"And you obviously failed your English lessons too." Cocoa admonished.

"I don't know what that woman's trying to say man. First off, she ain't got a mortgage and second of all, with all the money I lay on her, I for sure oughta own a piece of this place."

"Nothing in life is free, Negro. You want a free ride, go down and see Dicey at the firehouse. He hands them out to 'boys' like you all the time. You step up in this…"

– moving her hands from her hips to cross them across her breast.

"Ladies, ladies." Zak interrupted.

"Ah man, she knows she loves me, don't you sweet thang."

Intending to dismiss Thomas, Cocoa tossed her head, causing her ponytail to swing like a pendulum She headed to the kitchen for refills. She hadn't moved fast enough.

In one stride, Thomas caught up to her. In the next motion, from behind her, he had grabbed her right hand, spinning her around twice as if dancing, until she was facing him.

He let go the hand, caught her around the waist and carried her as easily as if she were a child the rest of the way to the kitchen.

His face never left hers as he sat her on the counter, trapping her there with his arms planted firmly on the counter on each side of her.

"If you don't let me go, you lunatic, I'll…"

"You'll what – gimme some of that…" Cocoa landed an open fist right along his jawline.

"You so nasty."

"Why you calling me nasty? All I was doing was asking you if you were gonna give me some of whatever ya'll drinking."

"And you're a liar to boot. Put me down." Thomas did but not until after taking her head in both hands and kissing her square on the mouth.

Kizzie and Zak smiled as they watched the sideshow going on in the kitchen. Trading interest in that show for the interest he had right now in Kizzie, Zak looked over to where she sat.

"Hey."

"Hey." She answered back.

"Hey doll."

"Hey you." She answered again.

Another game from their childhood. They had greeted each other the same way every day that she could remember. It made her feel as warm inside now as it had back then.

"Hey. You sure are a sight for sore eyes, you know that?"

Not really expecting an answer and without meaning to, Zak found himself back in a time and place almost forty years earlier.

As a young boy he had lived for the moment he would see her again, even if she had only been out of his sight for just a few minutes.

He could look at her for hours to make sure he never missed the instant something would tickle her and he would get to see her smile. And if it just happened that he was the one who caused her to be so happy he thought he was the luckiest person on the planet.

Back then his only ambition in life had been to give her a reason to smile.

He would follow her every where, whether she wanted him to or not. One time he remembered he must have been about ten and she was nine. It was during the summer.

Most of the time she liked having him around. He, Cocoa, the twins Solomon and Burke and Zak's friend Charlie would spend the whole day going from one adventure to another; fishing in the pond, climbing trees to see who could get the most apples without any falling to the ground, walking the trussel on the railroad tracks; playing dodge ball or some other scheme Zak and Charlie would hatch. Kizzie was right there in the middle of it all.

He would stop to watch her when she wasn't looking until she'd catch him at it. Depending on her mood she would smile and he would smile right back, feeling like he could die right then and be completely happy.

This day she wasn't in the mood for having him follow her around.

"If you don't stop following me, I'm gonna call the law on you for stalking me."

Zak figured she was just throwing around some big words from one of those books she was always reading.

"Go head call the law, cause I'll tell 'em, yeah I'm stalking her. But I'm really not stalking her. I just want to look at her. And if you follow me tomorrow, you'll see me stalking her again."

"You're crazy, Zak Bishop."

"Sure am. About you."

He would have traded his soul right then for the sound of her laughing. That was probably the first time he ever did his happy dance.

Zak let the memory fade as he focused back on what Kizzie was saying.

"I don't possibly see how I could be a sight for any eyes. After the way this day has gone, I feel like I've been rubbed on a wash board and wrung out like a rag. I must look a mess."

"You're just as pretty as ever."

Thomas' mumbled baritone interrupted whatever Zak had started to say next. Kizzie was so glad she could have kissed him.

"You two gonna finish up this card game tonight or you just gonna sit there grinning at each other?"

He had come back in from the kitchen holding a huge bag of chips between his teeth, two large bottles of beer in one hand and two mugs by the handles in the other.

Cocoa was on his heels with a large tray carrying the rest of the stuff, a big bowl of mixed nuts, more chips, a bottle of Smirnoff, one of Baccardi dark, cokes and a large pitcher of orange juice for the refills she had started on earlier.

She set the whole thing down on a side table alongside the ice bucket already in place.

"I think I'll go with the grinning at each other part." Zak said not taking his eyes off Kizzie.

"And I think Thomas ought to jump back into his own business and out of mine. Besides I was not grinning," Kizzie defended.

So here they were, still not finished with even one game because Cocoa hadn't been satisfied until she had nudged Zak into telling some of his ridiculous stories.

Still holding her sides and trying to catch her breath, Kizzie moaned, "Zak, stop. You ought to stop your lying".

"I swear to God it's true. But wait, let me tell you this one".

You know my father worked for old man Jessie down at the service station. Not the son who runs the place now but his father.

My father actually ran the garage for him. People would bring their cars in with all types of shit wrong with 'em and my father would fix them.

After he finished, he liked to take them out for a test drive. Now when my father tested a car, he would really test it. He might be gone for ten minutes or two days, you just never knew.

"He'd just take the people's car?" This from Cocoa.

"Swear to God."

So anyway, when he'd finally show back up, most of the time with no gas and who knows how many miles he'd put on it and people want to know where the hell he'd been with their car, my father would have the nerve to act mad.

"Well, I had to test the damn thing didn't I? What if I was to give you your car back and you get twenty miles down the road and it break down on you? Then your black ass would be back up in here wanting to cuss me out, talking 'bout how I took your money and didn't fix your car.

And see then my feelings would be hurt and I might not like it. I might have to kick some ass."

Don't you know half these people would actually thank him. The other half, who didn't like his bullshit but knew they couldn't do anything about it, would just look at him and walk away.

But they knew they wouldn't have any more problems with their car so they paid him and let him get away with it.

Now this one time…my father would bust his ass, all week long. Work like a dog. But come Friday night he was gonna have some fun. And whatever struck him to do at the time is what he would do."

Here the card game stops altogether because Kizzi, Cocoa and Thomas have all laid their cards face down on the table, set down their drinks and are paying close attention 'cause they know it's going to be a good one.

"So anyway, this one time, on a Friday night, my father showed up at my mothers to get me. I was only sixteen. "Homeboy". Let's go to Ladysmith's Homeboy".

I would tell him "Pop, Ladysmith's is five hundred miles from here and I'm not exactly flush with cash." And what you gone drive?

"I gotcha Homeboy, don't you worry 'bout what I'm gonna be driving. Let's go, let's go.

I walk outside and see this raggedy ass car that don't look like it's gonna make it around the block and back and he wants me to ride with him in this thing a thousand miles?!!!

"I don't know 'bout this shit Pop."

"Oh come on Homeboy, ride with me, it'll be alright!"

"Now, this isn't the first time I had been with him on one of these trips and if anything, the man was gonna have a good time. And if there was fun to be had, I was in.

So here we go. Ladysmith's is this one room juke joint, in this little town four states away and 'bout five miles back up in the woods.

No money to speak of, no change of clothes, no nothing but here we go. My father was born there and had been gone for years but still knew everybody and everybody still knew him, especially the women.

So we go down there and spend all Friday night and all Saturday. Finally on Saturday night we're on the way back. James Bishop is flying. That old ass car felt like it was gonna die any minute but my father kept giving it hell.

He must have been going well over a hundred miles an hour in that thing, passing everything in sight, talking and laughing his ass off.

Well, somehow he had let this woman talk him into hitching a ride back to the city to some relative of hers. I'd never seen her before.

All I know is she was a big woman. When she climbed in the back seat that car must have dropped three or four inches.

He was still half drunk, I'm still half drunk and who knows what the hell that woman in the back was.

We get 'bout halfway home, and we see these police headlights behind us. "Goddamn home boy. Hide that liquor, hide the guns!"

"Guns, what goddamn guns. You didn't tell me 'bout no guns!!

"Well, I figured I'd tell you if you needed to know."

"Now is a hellava time for you to make that decision."

"So I'm trying to stuff all these liquor bottles, full ones, empty ones, beer cans and all kinds of shit under the seat.

Damn Big James, don't you ever clean out this piece a shit car?" He rams this gun in my hand outta his damn belt that I hadn't even known he had and tells me to make sure I get the one outta the glove compartment too. In the meantime, I looked back at this woman in the back and she is stuffing shit everywhere...in her bra, under her dress, down in the seat. I'm thinking, sure as shit, we're going to jail."

Zak is now in full storytelling mode and has added the theatrics to go along with the words of the story.

He's pretending the couch is the car seat; flailing his hands wildly imitating to the other three what she looked like trying to find places to hide all this stuff.

He went from that to pushing his hand up and down his open shirt, then raising his butt up off the couch and moving his hands like he was the woman stuffing guns and cans up under her dress.

Thomas is rolling on the floor, Kizzi is dying on the couch and Cocoa is jumping up and down with her legs together like she's gonna piss any minute.

Zak can hardly keep it together himself. He finally recovers enough to finish the story.

"My father finally pulls over. The cop comes up to the car.

"License and registration please."

My father says "Well, that might be kind of hard officer, cause I don't have either one of those." He's got his elbow propped up on the window ledge so he can keep his hand over his mouth, hoping the cop won't smell the liquor.

"You don't have a license?

"No sir"

"Is this your car?"

"Well, not exactly Officer."

"Well, then whose car is it?

"I'm sort of test driving it for one of my customers. See, I'm a mechanic and that's what I do for a living".

"I see. Is that your customer in the back".

Now, ya'll should've seen this woman. She was already big but she had so much shit stuffed in her clothes she looked like she had three titties and with her legs gapped open to hide all that shit she stuffed up there her ass covered over half the back seat. She had this look on her face like she was scared to death. Her eyes were popping, she was wringing her hands and doing all kinds of twists with her mouth but no sound was coming out. The thing was, the way she was sitting in the seat, she could see my father's eyes dead set on her in the rear view mirror. She knew her ass better not say a word."

"No sir."

"The officer waits to see if my father is gonna volunteer any more of an explanation. That wasn't gonna happen. The one thing he always told me was "Homeboy, don't ever volunteer shit. I don't care if it's your woman, a cop or God herself, you don't ever volunteer any information".

After the cop figured out he wasn't volunteering any more info, he asked Big James.

"Where exactly is your customer?" In wherever city it was, my father says and tells him the name of the city.

"Sir, that happens to be more than two hundred and fifty miles away from here and you're test driving this car?"

"Yes sir officer, that's what I'm doing."

So now, the officer looks over at me. "Does he have a driver's license? I see him from the corner of my eye 'cause I am ramrod straight and my eyes are straight ahead. I'm thinking, "Oh Jesus, Oh Jesus, Oh Jesus"

"No sir".

The officer leans in and looks in the back. "So I guess it's probably useless for me to ask if she has one?"

"That would be an affirmative officer".

The officer looks at Big James like he wanted to ask him, where in the hell did you come up with that word.

"So let me get this right. I track you going a hundred and two, you have no license or registration, and nobody in the car has any license.

You want me to believe that you're test driving this vehicle and for all I know it might be stolen. Let me ask you, if you were in my place, what would you do with the three of you?"

Without missing a beat, my father says "I'd let me take my customer back his car. Cause he's gonna be mad as a motha fucka if you take this car and he has to come get it".

You could tell the officer was dumbfounded. It took him more than a few minutes to recover. Me and the woman just sat there and kept our mouths shut.

Finally, the officer says "You're either telling the truth or you're the biggest fool I've ever seen. Nobody but a fool would be out here with a car that looks like this one pushing it a hundred miles an hour. So I'm just gonna give you a warning. Get the hell outta here and slow your ass down before you kill somebody".

He didn't have to say it twice.

When I looked back the officer was leaning back against the hood of his car with his arms folded.

He was laughing so hard he looked like he was in pain.

Much later, Kizzie had managed to get herself upright on the couch.

Zak had moved from the couch back to the card table and sat with his legs stretched out underneath and his arms flung out, locked behind his head.

Thomas was trying to come up off the floor but had only been able to sit up with his back against the couch.

When Cocoa had stopped jumping up and down she leaned, knees bent, back straight with her head against the door frame to the kitchen which was now holding her upright. She had no strength to do it herself.

Deciding it was move or have to wipe up a puddle from the floor, she hauled ass off to the bathroom.

Gradually, they had each fumbled their way back to the card table. For more than half an hour after Zak finished the story, they all had tried hard to get their minds back into the Bid Whist game started much earlier in the evening.

But no sooner than the next hand was dealt and the bidding started, one of the group would look at another, it didn't matter which of them it was, the laughter would start again.

Or Zak, always the one to keep the fun going, would start the theatrics again, imitating what the woman in the car looked like trying to stuff her clothes.

By mutual agreement they decided this game would not be finished tonight.

Thomas and Zak talked while Zak shuffled the cards and put them back in the box.

Thomas folded the table and stacked it and the chairs back in the closet underneath the stairs. Kizzie and Cocoa reappeared after clearing the food and rinsing the dishes. "Just leave them there Kiz. I'll take care of them later."

"Thomas is going to take me over to pick up my car...Cocoa started to say.

Thomas interrupted..."then I'm taking my woman over to Stoney's and get our groove on for awhile out on the dance floor." He put both hands out in front of him, making L's at the elbows, snapping his fingers and moving his rear in and around like he was buttering a bowl.

"I don't know nothing about that being part of the plan." Cocoa declared.

"That's cause you hanging with Thomas baby. And Thomas always gotta have a plan." he fired right back, referring to himself in third person.

"Besides, you already told me you wanted Kizzie to get some rest so I'm gonna take you out so you don't have to wonder 'bout what you gon' do with yourself on a Friday night when it's still early."

"Your consideration for both of us overwhelms me." Turning to Kizzie she said "Hey, you two wanna come with us?"

"What I want to do right now is to bury myself so deep between those sheets I become one with the mattress. Don't worry about me. Go have a good time." It was all Kizzie could do to swallow the yawn.

"OK then. Let me just run freshen up a little. I'll be right back." Looking at Thomas,

"But I'm driving my own car.

"You gotta get to your car first suga." Thomas winked at Zak.

"Thomas Blackwell!"

"That's my name, Darlin'. Just put some clothes on woman, the night won't be young forever."

Handing Kizzie the box of cards, Zak started for the front door. "I guess I'll be going too. Let you get some rest. But let me ask you something. Outside of the five times you went back and forth out at Burning Cross, was the rest of your trip ok?" he asked, still in the mood for teasing.

"It was not five times and yes, the drive was fine. Just long."

Thomas was already outside, standing on the middle step finishing his cigarette when Cocoa bounced out the door, ready to go. Hi heels, just like the ones she'd worn earlier, except these were candy apple red; matching plain red tee shirt tied in a knot at her waist, and white jeans.

"You guys can lock up if you want. I've got keys." She stepped into the door of the 1975 baby blue Roadrunner GTO held open for her by Thomas. Without a thank you she slammed the door shut herself and waved from the window.

Thomas just shrugged his shoulders, smiling, as he took his seat behind the wheel. He also waved and they were gone.

Feeling just a bit nervous at being alone with Zak, she went the rest of the way down the steps when she felt his closeness behind her.

Zak stepped down and came up behind her again.

"Don't be such a chicken. I don't bite."

"I do."

"Same ole Kizzi."

"Same ole Zak."

Zak knew she must be tired. But he couldn't bring himself to leave her just yet. Not wanting to make her any more skittish than he could tell she was already, he walked the few paces it took to stand beside her Jeep under the carport off to the right of the house.

It's where the Mercedes would have been if Cocoa had brought it home. There were other spaces in the driveway that curved from the carport but Cocoa had insisted that Kizzie park there for the night.

"He must have asked her to marry him ten times." Zak nodded toward the fading taillights at the end of the long driveway.

Kizzie didn't know if he was talking to her or if he was just thinking out loud so she remained silent.

"Nice Jeep. I see your stuff is still in it. Want me to take it inside for you?" "No toll!

"Nah." I only needed the one suitcase tonight and Coe took that in earlier for me. The rest can wait. Thanks though."

"You're welcome."

He moved closer again, facing her. This time so close her nose was just inches away from the opening of his teeshirt. He leaned down and gently kissed her first on the left cheek, then did the same on the right. "Welcome home Precious." No response.

"You gonna talk to me or what."

"I have been talking to you."

He waited a minute.

"I'm glad you came home Kiz. I was hoping you would."

"Really? Why's that?"

"You know. I've wondered how you were, wanting to see you, find out why you left..."

"And what gives you the right to know those things?" Kizzie was getting angry all over again. "What is it you want from me Zak? You left me all those years ago. And not once did I hear a word from you. Not once! And now all of a sudden I'm supposed to act like everything is the same?"

She moved away from his closeness, again, determined she would bust a gut before she would let him see even one tear.

"It wasn't because I didn't want to Kizzie. I would have torn the world apart to find you but I couldn't have lived if you had told me you didn't want me in your life. I thought if I didn't see you I could just pretend things were like they were before. And you'd never have to know the truth."

"What truth Zak? The truth about the night I waited for you, all dolled up in my new dress it took hours of shopping to find...only to feel like a fool when I accepted that you had stood me up? Or the truth about how I was finally beginning to feel like I hadn't died along with my parents, then have it snatched out from under me. Or how about this truth? About whatever happened between you and Seal, the night you left town. I saw you with my own eyes after I ran all over town, in my new dress, looking for you. I'd waited hours for you to pick me up. Don't try to deny it." All the while she had been talking she was stabbing his chest with her finger. He had taken a step back with each poke and was now pressed against the door of her Jeep.

She was out of breath.

Zak was stunned. "You were there that night?"

"I was there. So don't bother trying to tell me how much you cared about me when she was the one you chose to tell good-bye. I let you make love to me Zak and it was so magical. I trusted you, like you asked me to. You said you loved me and would be here for me, always. Then you just up and left me without so much as a good-bye."

She couldn't stop. "That's love? It wasn't true then and it's not true now. Just save whatever story you think you can sell me on. Leave me alone!"

He had learned long ago never hang around for an argument you know you're going to lose. Another lesson from Big James.

She watched until the taillights of his old truck completely disappeared down the drive. In less than two minutes she was back up the steps, the house was locked, lights off and she had crawled in between those wonderful cool sheets. She was asleep before her heart finished saying "G'night Zak."

Chapter 8

She watched through one of the small panes of the French doors as the butterfly fluttered from petal to petal on the magnolia bush in her friend's back yard.

It was a black monarch dancing to a tune only it could hear. It would land on a petal, taste the nectar, start to fly away only to fly back again in a second or two.

She watched it perform the dance several times then move to the next petal and start all over again. It was as if it couldn't quite decide which petal had the sweetest juice and if it had tasted enough.

It was not yet dawn. The sun hovered just on the horizon as though it too, as indecisive as the butterfly, couldn't quite decide whether it wanted to rise any further today.

The sight of it gave promise to a perfect summer day; sunshine, warm and breezy. But at this early hour, the air was still cool.

Kizzie turned away from watching the butterfly. She wrapped both hands around the warm teacup, a mint she found exactly where she knew it would be in Cocoa's kitchen.

She had brewed enough for herself and Cocoa and washed the dishes left in the sink from the night before, then headed out to the porch.

She looked around her at the glass enclosed porch of the house she had practically grown up in. Except for a fresh coat of paint, thanks to Zak she was sure, and new cushions on the patio set, it was exactly as she knew it would be.

There were three sets of French doors. The one she had watched the butterfly through was dead center, much wider than the narrow ones at each of the side entrances. There were thirty two small glass panes in each door of this set and sixteen large panes in each door panel of the other two.

She knew, because as unbelievable as it was to her friend Cocoa, one of her favorite things to do as a child was to volunteer for the chore of polishing all those windows.

She loved it because when she was done she could sit for hours and watch as the sun beamed rays of light through them that made beautiful patterns of color on the waxed wood floors.

She would conjur up those images years later in the creative arts work she did as part of her job as Executive Director for the Vice President of the firm where she worked.

It was a long porch, covering the full length of the back of the house. There were long panels of glass from the center French door around the wall to each of the side ones.

They started at the eaves just beneath the roof and met a half wall of bead board that enclosed the bottom half.

Along the back wall as you entered from the kitchen door was an enormous wicker sofa, white with soft cushions covered in bright bold colors, red and white.

Two matching rockers sat across from it on the other side of the kitchen door, same cushions.

Huge, healthy ferns hung at each corner and glass topped wicker coffee and side tables sat all over.

Two large ceiling fans ran twenty four hours a day. Even though air conditioners had recently been installed in this section of the porch, it was rarely necessary to have it turned on.

If you ventured out either of the side doors you would follow the wrap around until it ended at the front portion of the porch. But what fun you would find along the way!

There was hand painted art work and figurines on the walls and floor, a lot of which Kizzi had sent to Cocoa's parents from wherever in the world she happened to be. Huge ceramic pots of blooming Sweet Williams and hibiscus were mixed in with tall cacti that must have been as old as Cocoa.

From the side doors at the back porch to the front was screened in from top to bottom. Stepping off at the front porch steps you could follow a trail of purple verbena spreading out from a wide bed of white stones, ending at the back porch again.

At night she and Cocoa, Seal and her brothers, and Zak used to find their favorite spot on this porch to sit and listen to Kizzie's Mom tell one of her stories.

Lizzie Carpenter had been a wonderful storyteller and everyone, grown-ups and children alike, would sit mesmerized as she talked.

Kizzie remembered, even now, how her voice would change in cadence with the story- sometimes low so that they would have to lean in close so as not to miss a word; other times it would rise and fall, then fast and slow, sometimes short, quick sentences or one word would be drawn out so long that when she finally released it you would find yourself exhaling when you didn't even know you had been holding your breath.

Kizzie's favorite spot had been next to her mother where she could put her head in her lap. She'd soak in the smell of her, chicken fried for dinner or the smell of soap from having just washed the dishes.

Kizzie had never felt more loved and safe and as hard as she would try not to, would almost always fall asleep and miss the end of the story.

"It was a wonderful childhood, wasn't it Sis?"

Kizzie was not startled at the sound of her friend's voice or at the feel of her arms as Cocoa wrapped them around her shoulders, enveloping her from the back.

Cocoa's height allowed her to stand close behind Kizzie. She draped one arm down each shoulder and crossed them tightly just beneath Kizzie's chin.

"Hmm, the best." Kizzie answered. She reached up with both her hands to hold Cocoa's crossed ones. "I was just remembering how Ma used to tell us stories until we'd fall asleep right where we were. She'd just cover us with a blanket, the whole bunch of us, and we would wake up out here in the morning."

"Or, Cocoa added, when she'd tell one of those ghost stories, 'haints', as Zak still calls them, and we'd be too scared to move, holding onto the skirts or pants legs of whatever grown-up happened to be near us."

They both laughed at the memory. Kizzie's thoughts had gone to Zak when Cocoa mentioned 'haints' but she decided to put them away until a later time.

"I made tea."

"Hmm, I smelled it all the way upstairs. That's how I knew you were up and out here."

Cocoa unfolded her arms from around Kizzie's neck, kissing her on the top of her head, and walked over to where Kizzie had stood earlier watching the butterfly.

"You still have that old thing?" This from Kizzie when she got a glimpse of what Cocoa was wearing; baggy red, short sweats and a white tee shirt with the words ' I Will Always Strive to Make My Mother Proud' written across the front.

"Sure do and I bet you do too." Right again. Kizzie had packed it in her suitcase the day before.

They laughed again at another shared memory. At the time they bought the tee shirts, it was not their mothers they were thinking of with pride.

It had been Kizzie's fourteenth birthday and Cocoa's twelth. The same birthday was just one of the things they had in common. What was ironic was that there were just as many that they disagreed vehemently about – the subject of men being one and their strongest.

As with any other girl in that age bracket, their conversations were dominated with the idea of growing breasts. Being mortified at the thought of saying the word out loud, their pet name for them had become 'trimbles'. No one knew why.

This particular birthday, they were elated. There were sure signs that the long wait was over. Having made the discovery while getting dressed that morning at Kizzie's house where Cocoa had spent the night in anticipation of the big day, they proudly marched down the steps and out the door in search of their mothers.

Miss Lizzie and Miss Mazie Sullivan, also the best of friends, were on this very porch, only four houses down from the Carpenters.

They had just arrived back from gathering vegetables from the garden they shared on a corner lot provided by the town but adjacent to the back of the Sullivan's property.

Their haul today included fresh dug potatoes, ripe tomatoes, butterbeans and yellow squash. They were sitting each in one of the rockers with their aprons full of butterbeans they needed to shell for supper later that day.

Hands full of butterbeans, Miss Lizzie used her knee to hunch Miss Mazie when she noticed the girls come around the corner. "Wanna try to guess what's up with those two?"

"I'm sure whatever I came up with wouldn't even come close," Miss Mazie declared. At least they look too clean still for Cocoa to have been in a fight so early. But would you get a load of that walk. This is gonna be gooood!"

Knowing their girls and their habit of getting into any number of things they weren't supposed to, they both in silent agreement decided to wait to hear this latest before they said anything.

The girls continued their march, side by side; Cocoa younger but already much taller than Kizzie, standing straight as an arrow, heads held high, chests stuck out.

Choosing not to take the wrap around from the front of the house they walked along the outside of the house on the worn path that ran parallel to the verbena.

Climbing the wide steps up to the French doors, they waited until they were standing directly in front of their mothers.

"We need bazzieres for our trimbles." they both proclaimed in unison.

"What!" the mothers yelled, also in unison.

"We finally got our trimbles and now we need brazzieres," from Kizzie in a voice high in urgency and anxiety.

It took a few seconds of looking from their daughters' faces to the raised bumps the size of small plums on their chests to get the full picture.

When comprehension dawned, they both quickly lowered their heads to their chests in an attempt to squash the laughter bubbling to the surface and sure to explode if they didn't maintain some control.

Miss Lizzie was banging Miss Mazie with her knee and Miss Mazie was doing the same to Miss Lizzie.

They were both squirming in their rockers, arms folded across their guts, trying desperately not to dump the beans they had worked so hard on from their aprons, while they came up with something to say that would not cause them to double over in laughter.

"Wellllllllllll" Cocoa moaned.

"Well what, dear," her mother answered, still not making eye contact.

"Maaaaaaaaaa," Kizzie whailed, hardly able to contain herself. "We need to go to the store, right now. We can't walk around like this with our trimbles out, not now that we are women. What would people say?"

That did it!

Miss Lizzie, body bobbing up and down in the rocker as she was bursting silently inside, put her right elbow on the rocker's arm, raised her hand to cover her mouth as she turned her head to the left to whisper to Miss Mazie, "If we laugh out loud, they will never forgive us."

All Miss Mazie could do was bob her head as she tried to look anywhere but directly at the girls, and those chests!

Finally managing to regain some level of composure, Miss Lizzie said "Well, what would people think indeed?"

It took a minute but having gotten at least enough to be able to talk they had promised the girls that if they would help them finish getting the vegetables washed and shelled, and being it was their birthdays, they would make sure to take them to the store that very day.

Needless to say color, size, texture and how many was the topic for the entire trip.

After the final selection of two each from Mr. Bloom's limited selection for girls of that age, Kizzie spotted a row of tee shirts along the back wall they hadn't seen before.

Convincing their mothers that the tee shirts would be perfect birthday presents, they took their selections to the dressing room.

Wanting to display their womanhood by any means, they both had taken the very smallest sizes they could find.

Emerging from the dressing room, the tee shirts tight across their trimbles, which read 'I Will Always Strive to Make my Mother Proud', but barely reaching their waistlines, they looked right into the faces of their mothers.

They were holding the same tee shirts but in the very largest size they could find. They were so large the girls would wear them for years like dresses.

"We know you will always make us proud dears." Miss Lizzie said, in the tone all too familiar to Kizzie and Cocoa as the one that meant you didn't put up any further argument.

With that, they paid the clerk and walked from the store, the girls with their own bags, right behind, so excited about their treasures, even the thought of wearing huge tee shirts couldn't dampen their spirits.

That had been almost thirty years ago and they were still wearing those tee shirts.

Chapter 9

"I didn't hear you come in last night. You have a good time?"

"Oh, we had a great time, girl. Stoney's was packed and all the buzz was about little Kizzie Carpenter. I thought I was going to have to slug somebody. They wanted to tar and feather me because I had the nerve to show up without you."

"I don't know why everybody has their draws in knots because of me! I was born and raised in this town just like all of them."

"Yeah, but you're the small town girl who went off and did good. They're proud of you. Everybody had some story to tell about how they knew you. And the more they drank the bigger their stories got. One trying to outdo the one before. Girl, you should've heard some of them. By the time the night was over anybody who didn't have a story just made up a great big lie, just to be a part of it all." Cocoa laughed as she walked back into the kitchen to reheat her tea. "I don't think Stoney has ever seen that much excitement at his place."

"Is that the same Old Man Stoney who had the place when we were growing up? He must be what... eighty years old by now?"

"Close. Seventy eight. And still opens and closes that place every Thursday, Friday and Saturday night. Thomas is the DJ there on the same nights. He and Zak helped Stoney add on to the place about eight, ten years ago. Since it's the only place in town to have any real fun, he needed the extra space. But people still hang out on the porch just like we used too. He's added tables in the back where we used to dance in the grass. With lights strung from the ceiling in those paper lanterns...it's real nice. From Sunday to Wednesday, it's a hangout for the kids after school. Boys from the local high school come in to shoot pool but mostly shoot BS to the girls. Maybe we'll get a chance to take you in and show your stuff one night before you leave."

"Well, you might have more chances than you think." Kizzie finished her tea and set the cup down on the glass top of one of the side tables next to the rocker where she sat.

It was the one her mother used all those years ago. Cocoa took the other one.

"Yeah, I noticed you packed a little bit more than a person might need for a weekend in this town. Even for you." I'm like damn! This girl really likes to change clothes. That, or there's just a little more to this trip than she's let on."

"I don't know what came over me Coe. At first I wasn't the least bit excited about coming back here again. So I had waited until the last minute before I even thought about packing. Then when I got started it was like I was being drawn back here. I couldn't wait. I was standing in the middle of my bedroom and it dawned on me that after all the time and effort I had put into my life in the city, I still didn't feel like I belonged there. I felt tired of it all...the job I worked so hard at, the townhouse I was so proud of...it just didn't feel like home anymore. Next thing I know, I'm packing up everything I can stuff into the Jeep, closing up the house and here I am. And I have absolutely no idea what I'm going to do after this weekend. Do you know I haven't thought about Marcus once since I left?"

Cocoa waited for Kizzie to go on. She watched her rock back and forth. Because she knew Kizzie as well as she knew herself she knew there would be nothing else forthcoming at the moment.

Pressing her now for more info would be a waste of time.

"And you know what? You don't have to think about him now or any of it for that matter. Your room is still upstairs as always and you're home here for as long as you want."

Cocoa had sensed during the ride home in the Jeep that something was troubling her friend. She knew Kizzie would get around to telling her in her own way and in her own time.

71

Way back when they were just girls, Cocoa's real father George Sullivan, had made them a 'playhouse' out of the room underneath the stairs.

The same closet where Thomas stashed the card table the night before. It was a huge space and it became their own special place. It was filled with their favorite playthings, dolls and stuffed animals. Their mothers gave them lots of their old clothes and shoes and make-up bags that they used for dress up.

But mostly it was filled with their little girl secrets and confessions, little things they vowed to never breathe to another living soul. Cocoa couldn't count the number of times Kizzie would grab her hand and drag her into that closet. At those times there was always a great sense of urgency so Cocoa would have to drop whatever it was she was doing to hear the latest secret or giggle at the latest taboo topic.

It had been their place of comfort when Cocoa would cry from being teased about her hair or Kizzie from being called high yellow.

The last time they had used that closet was the day Kizzie was told her parents were dead and it hit her that she would never see them again. That's when everyone started to call it Kizzie's Closet. As much time as they had spent there, this was the one time everyone seemed to remember.

Cocoa had stayed with her that day for hours. Dress up was forgotten, there was no interest in any of the playthings or giggling at silly teenage gossip. She sat on the large pillow with her back against the wall. Kizzie was curled up in a fetal position with her head on Cocoa's lap.

Cocoa had never heard anyone cry with such agonizing pain. She had never heard anyone since. It was the one and only time in her life she had ever felt utterly and completely helpless.

So she did the only thing she could. She sat in silence, hour after hour, listening to her best friend purge her pain through her tears. Her right arm that was under Kizzie's head had long ago become numb but she didn't care. With her left she simply stroked Kizzie's hair, almost wringing wet from her own tears.

Eventually Cocoa's mother had forced her to come out, at least to try to eat. Kizzie refused to budge.

She was there for two days, never leaving except to go to the bathroom. On the third day she came out to attend her parents' funerals. She hadn't been in there again since that day.

It wasn't until years after Kizzie had left town that Cocoa helped her mother clean out the closet to use it for more storage.

"And when you're ready, I'll be here for you. We'll just go sit in Kizzie's Closet like we used to and laugh or cry our way through it just like we've always done."

"Oh Cocoa, Kizzie's Closet! I had almost forgotten about it. I can't believe all the stuff we used to talk about and do in that room.

I think that's where you first fell in love with hi heeled shoes. Remember how many times you'd fall when you practiced walking. We used to play dress up for hours. Zak used to be mad because we would never tell him what we were doing and wouldn't let him come in." Kizzie's voice lost its cheerfulness.

Cocoa didn't have to wonder why. She simply reached over the arm of the rocker and held her friend's hand.

"But no matter what it was, we always felt like we could solve the world's problems right in that room, didn't we? I missed having that after you left. But you're here now and we're going to have a great time. Say, speaking of Zak, how long did he hang around after Thomas and I left?"

"Oh just long enough to let me know that he knew he could still get under my skin."

Kizzie quickly switched subjects. "And speaking of Thomas...Girl, from all the times you've told me how ugly he was, I couldn't believe that was him last night. I don't see why you think he's so ugly. I think he's a good looking guy. He's just got that funny looking eye but he's still not bad looking at all. You've got funny looking hair but I still think you're beautiful!"

She leaned back in the rocker to duck the smack she knew Cocoa was going to take at her for mentioning the 'funny hair' in the way the kids used to tease her when they were kids. "He's obviously crazy about you."

"Well, he had cleaned up some last night. He knew I would've murdered his black ass if he'd come stepping up in here to meet my best friend wearing them sweaty bib overalls, no shirt and them dirty brogain boots. Girl! He knew better."

"Coe, the man is a housing contractor. He fixes houses and paints for a living. What do you expect him to dress like?"

"Well, all I can say is he knows he better clean up his act big time when he heads my way, 'cause Cocoa don't play that. But what can I say...he loves me."

"He really does Coe. And I'm so happy for you. So does that mean you're becoming an exclusive?"

Cocoa raised both hands, palms out as if warding off a curse. "I'm not saying all that now. The jury's still out. Oh Kiz, I'm so so happy to have you home."

They sat for another few minutes. Words weren't needed.

Cocoa rose first and moved to stand inside the kitchen door. "Hey, I've gotta get dressed. I've got a ton of things to do still down at the luncheon. We've got another big day ahead."

"Oh shit, Cocoa, what now? Don't you think it would be nice to let me in on my own agenda since everybody else in this town seems to know better than I do what I'm supposed to be doing and when?"

"Actually, there's not THAT much today!

Somewhere around eleven thirty or so I'm supposed to bring you over to Hillside Park for lunch. It's a picnic in your honor and the whole town is invited.

The Ladies Auxiliary thought they should do their part to celebrate the town's Shero. And being that the Mayor didn't want to piss them off, otherwise he'd have hell to pay with their husbands on any council meeting for the next hundred years, he was persuaded to let them put on this luncheon for you. You, my dear

Kizzie, will be presented with the first and only key to the city."

"Oh my God Cocoa. You've got to be kidding. You know I hate that kind of fuss. And so do you. I can't believe you let yourself get talked into taking part in this, this..." Kizzie was at a loss for just what to call it.

"Well, uh, to be honest, uh, it was uh, uh kind of me doing the talking."

Cocoa struggled getting the truth past her tongue and off her lips. She lifted her head to gaze at the ceiling as if she was looking for cracks; anything to avoid eye contact with Kizzie.

Kizzie had lowered her head almost to her chin with it leaning to the side. She had her hands on her hips and her eyes were lifted at Cocoa without lifting her head. A look Cocoa knew well. "I simply do not believe you sometimes, Ms. Sullivan."

Getting past the moment, she turned back to face Kizzie square on.

"Oh come on girl! You've done a wonderful thing for this town. Everybody, and I do mean everybody knows that if it weren't for you, this place wouldn't even be a dot on the local map. I simply reminded them of that AND the fact that you've actually given them back their livelihoods. The people here like to pay their debts and they owe you big time. Don't take away the chance for them to show you their gratitude, Kiz, and don't sell yourself short either. Just shut up and let them do this in their own little half ass way."

Kizzie just continued to look at her. If she knew her for another fifty years, Cocoa would always find ways to amaze her.

"I'm going to get dressed. I'll be back for you around eleven. And don't you dare touch the stuff in your Jeep. Solomon and Burke will be over about mid morning to take everything upstairs to your room. See ya."

A quick hug, kiss on the forehead and ten seconds later she was alone again.

Chapter 10

Kizzie sat where she was, taking a deep breath as if breathing in would add a measure of reality to the past forty eight hours. She still was shocked at the idea of a whole town putting on it's best face for her...the celebration yesterday, being presented with a key to the city today and Monday another celebration!

She didn't believe what she had done was that extraordinary. Even though this hadn't been her home in years, it was her hometown and she loved it.

The people here were hard working, mostly farmers who raised cotton, tobacco and peanuts; decent human beings who cared deeply about family and friendships, the roots of which could be traced back for years.

She had simply been in a position to help and had snatched the option without a second thought. Anyone in her position would have done the same given the same set of circumstances.

She would never in a million years have dreamed it would generate this outpouring of gratitude. It was very humbling. She thought about Cocoa's last words to her. She took several more deep breaths and as she exhaled she made up her mind that she would be more gracious in accepting their thanks.

Rising from the rocker, she went through the narrow French doors to her left and out onto the wrap around. Several feet later, she stopped to run her hands across the three painted ceramic squares made of stone that she had sent to Cocoa as a housewarming gift when she bought the place from her mother.

They were painted in earth tones of blues, greens and browns, each one twelve by twelve inches with rough surfaces. She had bought them from a roadside stand on the Indian Reservation in South Dakota where she was sent on her first land research assignment.

The trio represented the elements of nature that the Indians believed were required to keep life in balance – fire, wind and water. Each one was signed by a Lakota (Sioux) Indian child, then with the word – **tiyospaye-** (tie yo spay) meaning love for the extended family.

Kizzie had a Dreamcatcher made in the same colors hanging from the mirror in her bedroom. It was a plate, two inches long and one inch wide, made of sterling silver. Inside was carved a circle of twisted feathers. Inside the circle was a web similar to several connected hexagons. Three feathers had been carved to hang from the bottom edge of the circle. According to Legend, good dreams pass through the center hole to the sleeping person. Bad dreams are trapped in the web, where they perish in the light of dawn.

Taking the steps down from the porch she followed the trail of purple verbena toward the front of the house. Just before reaching the front the path curved to the right and gave way to another short driveway that led to the front yard of an old carriage house.

When she was growing up it had been a huge storage shed that her mother and Miss Mazie had used as a pantry. Each summer, Kizzie, Cocoa, Zak, Solomon and Burke, Seal and any number of other children who could be found underfoot at either the Carpenters or the Sullivans, were sent to gather bushels of vegetables from the garden.

It would take all summer but by the time fall arrived there would be hundreds of jars of canned tomatoes, beans, peaches, squash, pickled cucumbers and watermelon, jellies, jams and all kinds of preserves lined up on row after row of shelves. There would be bins overflowing with sweet potatoes, white potatoes, onions, peanuts and corn.

Kizzie closed her eyes. The feeling of nostalgia was so intense she could actually smell the scent of those wonderful fruits as they bubbled in huge pots on the kitchen stove. The waves of homesickness caught her by surprise. She breathed in deeply again to ward off the tears.

After Miss Lizzie's death, Miss Mazie didn't enjoy canning as much. She missed the joy it had brought to her and her best friend.

She had moved all the leftover jars of vegetables and preserves into the pantry in the house. Her husband

George had converted it into a carriage house but she had never completely furnished it.

It had remained that way until Cocoa bought the property from her mother and spent the next six months brow beating Zak and Thomas into helping her convert it into a day care center. It was now a thriving business that she called 'Little Fingers'.

She would tell anyone in the world that she owed it all to Kizzie.

Kizzie looked at the name of the center, written in curvy letters, each a different color against a backdrop of white clapboards, along the top of the entrance above the door. A set of tiny hands were painted underneath.

Leave it to Cocoa.

This was a perfect business for her. She loved children but never had any of her own. So five days a week she cared for any number of preschool and after school children while their parents worked from sun up to sun down trying to make a living by picking the cotton, thrashing hay and peanuts and curing tobacco.

They arrived as early as six in the morning and were there until as late as nine at night. Sometimes later. Cocoa never charged their parents anything more than her standard eight hour daily rate and never turned anyone of them away.

On opening day she had just two children. But like anything else she set her mind to, Cocoa had thrown every ounce of energy into making it work. Now on any given day the place was running over with kids.

She made sure they had three meals a day, were challenged with games and learning aids and got plenty of play and exercise. But most of all she made sure they felt loved and safe.

Kizzie pushed open the front door and giggled at the sound of chimes playing the tune of Rock-A-Bye Baby. She found herself humming along since the chimes didn't stop when the door was closed but continued until the full course was completed.

All around her were walls of books and board games.

The walls were painted in bright bold blues and yellows and covered with artwork done by the children.

The small tables and chairs had been pushed back against the wall. A huge colorful rug with blocks of color in the same bold blue and yellow as the walls covered the center of the hardwood floor.

Soft pillows lay scattered on top of the rug. Toys and stuffed animals that hadn't made it back to the toy boxes lay scattered among the pillows.

Kizzie could imagine how happy a child would be just being in this room.

After several minutes she took one of the books from the shelf and sat down at one of the small tables lined against the wall.

The little chair was just high enough for her to slide her legs underneath the table. The book was an oversized volume of children's stories.

Kizzie flipped through the pages, stopping on 'The Old Lady Who Lived in the Shoe'. There was a picture of a boot filling the page. It was drawn to look like a house.

There were cut outs in the shoe that looked like windows with curtains. Children peeked out from everywhere.

She picked up a large crayon from the box on the table. As if her fingers had a mind of their own, they colored in her mother's name at the top of the boot.

Kizzie held the book open with both hands. She leaned back in the chair, resting her head against the bookcase, eyes focused on her mother's name, LIZZIE.

She had always loved it that her name rhymed with her mother's. After all these years she still missed her terribly. She had loved both her parents intensely but her Mama was special.

She closed her eyes again, as she often did, to let images of her Mom float across her mind's eye as though she were counting sheep.

She hadn't intended it but she was soon asleep, trails of dried tears on her face. She was unaware of the wet stains which dotted the front of the tee shirt she still wore from last night.

Chapter 11

He was straddling the ladder back chair as he sat across from her watching her sleep. His legs were so long that when he folded them his knees actually touched the floor.

He was perched more on them than the tiny chair. She obviously had not heard him come in so he was careful not to wake her.

He had bent down, no, practically laid on his stomach on the floor, to get another look at those legs he had only had a chance to glance at when he had pulled her over.

He smiled at the thought that she must still be pissed about that.

This was his Kizzie. He could sit there and watch her for hours. If this was as close to heaven as he ever got, he would die a happy man.

Except for the stylish, modern haircut instead of two long plaits and the addition of about five pounds that had settled in all the right places, she had changed little in all the years she had been absent from his life.

She was still light skinned except there were signs of a year round tan that gave her skin the glow of nicely browned toast. Not a wrinkle anywhere. The skin around arms that peeked out from the sleeveless tee shirt was nice and tight against her muscles. She didn't have Cocoa's striking beauty but beautiful she was.

He had never known anyone more beautiful; it radiated from her warmth, her fierce independence and self confidence, her loyalty to her friends and her love of life. At least that was the Kizzie he remembered.

He wasn't at all certain this was the Kizzie he saw as he sat looking at her.

He had tiptoed up behind her when he first came in and saw the book. His eyes focused on the dried tears on her cheeks. Seeing her mother's name across the top of the boot, he understood the tears.

He, like Cocoa had earlier, sensed a sadness in her that they had never seen before. His instincts told him that he was also partly responsible for her sadness.

He didn't know how long her visit was going to be this time but as he watched her he made a promise to himself. He would make up to her for whatever part he had played in dimming the sparkle in her eyes; the one that at one time had been brighter than the sun. "I swear to you, Miss Lizzie. I'll find a way to make her happy."

Her Jeep was crammed with her personal things so he knew she would be here for a while at least. However long that turned out to be, he hoped it would be enough to give him a head start.

The rest of it would take the balance of his lifetime. He would gladly dedicate every minute to putting back the joy he knew had been snatched from her, one painful jerk at a time.

He loved her. It was as simple as that. From the depth of his soul he loved her. He had from the moment he first saw her and knew without a doubt that it would never ever change. He didn't care.

She was so much a part of him that loving her was as natural as breathing. His friends still teased him about her. They called him obsessed to love someone who, for all intents and purposes, may as well have been a ghost, since he hadn't seen her in years.

He responded with no hesitation that he was and wouldn't change it for any amount of money or anything else in this universe.

Call him obsessed! Call him a fool! Call him crazy…he still didn't care! He would scream it to the world. Most of all he wanted to scream it to her.

He knew she had known it at one time. He also knew she had felt the same way about him. Back then it was a sure thing. Whether she still did was not so certain.

But he was willing to find out. He had never been afraid to bet on a long shot. This just happened to be the only time that his life, his happiness, his very survival would be his stake in the game.

She had been eighteen the last time he saw her; the year after her parents' death. They had been inseparable as children, already almost ten years ago.

There was nothing they hadn't shared with each other and there were never any secrets. They were as comfortable swimming naked in the lake together as they were fully clothed, sitting beside each other at the dinner table.

They were too young to put a label on their relationship; whether it was sister and brother, childhood friends or something else without a name.

Whatever the label, it was as clear to him now as it had always been. This was a once in a lifetime bond, given birth by Fate. And nurtured by a Power much greater than either of them could imagine.

He remembered the first day he had met her and that last day he had seen her as clearly as if it happened only moments ago. That first day he had known he would love her for life, that last day he had broken her heart.

No amount of time in a lifetime would ever be enough to let him forget that. Given a choice he would have driven a stake through his own heart instead.

Chapter 12

Zak had been raised mostly by his mother, Carrie Bishop. His father, Big James, had left when he was eight, just before Zak met Kizzie, Cocoa and their families.

Rumor had it that Miss Carrie cared more about sleeping with a man named Jack Daniels who came in a bottle than she did about sleeping with James Bishop. Jack was the first thing on her mind when she crawled out of bed in the mornings and the last thing on it when she fell into a drunken stupor at night.

Rumor also had it that Big James loved his son. He had made it clear in no uncertain terms that if he ever found out that she used the money he sent her for rent, bills and Zak's clothes to buy liquor, that he would kick her ass six ways from Sunday and all the way to West Bubblefuck.

So Miss Carrie managed to stay sober while she put in several hours a day down at Miss Suzie's House of Hair to buy food for her and Zak, but mostly to keep her supply of Jack Daniels at full level.

Not that she didn't drink at all while she worked! Everyone in the beauty shop was pretty sure that those trips to the back room weren't just to pick up more shampoo and hair grease. But say what you wanted about Miss Carrie.

The one thing that couldn't be criticized was the way she could turn out a head. The woman could lay some press and curls and just about every woman in town would gladly ignore her drinking to have her do her thang on their hair.

But as soon as the hair was swept up from the floor and the hot comb and curlers put away, she would head straight home to her friend 'Jack'.

She would call Zak to come home from the neighbor's, Miss Nellie, who babysat him after school. Sometimes she would tell him to get off the bus at the beauty shop and walk home with her. He had liked those days.

Then they would eat whatever was leftover in the refrigerator. Zak was never in a hurry to get home since most days the leftovers would be leftovers from the leftovers. Much of the time he wasn't there at all.

Even though he was only eight he was already tall for his age and seemed much older. So instead of playing in the back yard like Miss Nellie told him, he would pretend to be an explorer and roam the neighborhood.

He used to walk until Big James showed up one day with the prettiest bike Zak had ever seen. His father stayed around long enough to teach him how to ride it, then he was on his own again.

The bike turned out to be a second hand one and not as pretty as Zak first thought. Actually, it was a piece of shit bike Zak found out later. It was impossible to keep air in the tires and the handle bars had to be tightened constantly.

But to Zak, it meant freedom. He had wheels. He was mobile. He was never without that bike.

One day he rode it into town to surprise his mother at Miss Suzie's. He knew she would be mad but he liked being around her at work before she had a chance to get really drunk. She would stay mad for a little while, then she would hug him to her and call him her little man.

That was the first time he saw Kizzie and the last time he had owned his heart.

Miss Suzie was Seal's mother and Miss Mazie's sister. That's how Seal and Cocoa were cousins.

Miss Mazie would come into the beauty shop every two weeks to have her sister work her magic on her hair. The beauty shop sat on a corner lot at the edge of town.

Coming around the corner as Kizzie had done, it would be the first building on your left as you entered town.

It was an older, one story house; Miss Suzie lived in the back but had turned the two front rooms into her beauty parlor.

The house sat back several yards from the sidewalk with a gravel driveway and untended grass in the front yard. One step up would put you on the narrow porch that was filled with green plants and flower pots. A pink awning stretched from one end to the other and Miss Suzie's House of Hair was written in cursive white letters across the face of it.

Miss Lizzie and Kizzie had accompanied Miss Mazie the day he saw her. Cocoa was inside with Miss Mazie, who thought that being only four, Cocoa was too young to play outside that close to the end of town where she would not be able to watch out for her.

Kizzie, who was six, wasn't having it.

She loved being with her mother but being cooped up in that one room smelling fried hair held no attraction for her whatsoever.

So she was sitting on the stoop with a book, 'Fun with Dick and Jane'.

She had no shoes on and as she concentrated on the book, she rubbed her big toes in the dirt at the edge of the porch.

This was her first year of school and she had fallen in love with reading. Mr. Young, down at the grocery, had given the book to her the day she and her mother had stopped in for seeds for the garden.

Kizzie had been so excited by all the books she had seen in the library she had just gone on and on about how many there were. Mr. Young was impressed by her enthusiasm and had given her the book with the condition that she read the entire book and then come back to tell him about it. It had been with her each day since.

Zak rode his bike through the gravel up to the porch and stopped sideways in front of her, his legs dangling from the high seat.

'I'm Zak."

"I know that. I see you on the bus."

"Well, I didn't see you before," Zak said, at the same time wondering how he could have missed her. "What's your name?"

"Kizzie."

"Kizzie what?"

"Zak what?"

"Bishop."

"Carpenter."

"Wanna ride my bike?"

"I don't know how. Besides, it's too big for me."

"It's easy. I'll show you. Come on."

They both walked back through the gravel to the sidewalk, him pushing the bike along praying that the tires wouldn't go flat from the gravel and make him look really stupid.

Zak was a good teacher and Kizzie a good pupil. She had caught on quickly.

She fell only once, scrapping the skin off of one knee. The sight of her blood caused his eight year old heart to skip several beats.

He was by her side almost before she hit the ground, the bike forgotten. He helped her up, got down on his knees to brush the dirt from her clothes, then did the only thing he knew to do.

He took a handful of spit and wiped at her knee until the blood was completely gone.

The bond was sealed and solid. They became inseparable. And since Kizzie and Cocoa were inseparable, they soon became a trio. Rarely did you see one without the other two.

But the day Zak met Cocoa was entirely different from the day he met Kizzie. While meeting her had caused his heart to stop and his feet want to dance, meeting Cocoa had been cause for pain and humiliation.

Although she was only four and a half, she like Zak, was tall for her age. She had been raised around a bunch of male cousins and had learned early how to be a little scrapper.

This, combined with a personality that was already willful and headstrong, made her mentally strong and tough as nails. Miss Mazie had already accepted that she was going to be the tom boy of all tom boys.

She was playing jacks with Kizzie on the Caprenter's front porch. The Carpenter house was four houses down from the Sullivan's and he already loved spending time there.

It was a picture book house Zak thought; single story sitting high off the ground, white with blue shutters, made by Mr. Dallas, Kizzie's father. Miss Lizzie had seen a house with those shutters in a magazine at Miss Suzie's and thought their house would look so much nicer with them added to it.

The other houses in town just had painted frames around the windows so Mr. Dallas didn't understand what his wife had gotten so excited about. But if blue shutters was what she wanted, then blue shutters she got.

The porch was made of cement, also painted blue and sanded to a smooth surface. All the kids loved to play jacks there because the smooth surface meant their hands wouldn't get scratched when they swiped up the jacks. That could make or break their game.

The kids also knew that Miss Lizzie always had lots of food. Anyone who was there when it was time to eat got fed along with her family. So on any given day there were plenty of them around.

Today it was just Kizzie and Cocoa.

A wide swing hung on one end of the porch and a patio set, much like Miss Mazie's, sat on the opposite end.

Being high off the ground, there were ten steps leading down to the ground. White lattice work framed the crawl space and covered it and the bottom of the house from view.

The grass in the yard was well tended and recently cut.

It had been almost a week since he had met Kizzie.

He had started to look for her on the bus. She always saved a seat for him, threatening anyone who even looked liked they wanted to take the seat beside her.

Since Miss Nellie would tell Miss Carrie if he didn't take the bus home, he would go into the house as soon as he got off the bus, change his clothes, then head directly out the back door.

He would be at Kizzie's house within thirty minutes.

Miss Lizzie and Kizzie were never surprised to see him. He was becoming an everyday fixture at the Carpenter house. There was usually a place for him at the supper table and afterwards he and Kizzie would play until long past time for him to go home.

Sometimes Mr. Dallas would insist that he go home to check in with his folks. No sooner than they would think he was already home, Mr. Dallas would look up and there he would be again, back out playing with Kizzie.

Zak had learned that if he didn't come in until it was already dark, Miss Lizzie wouldn't let Mr. Dallas chase him home. "That boy shouldn't be running around in the dark by himself, she'd say and Zak would revel in the way she took up for him. Mr. Dallas simply shook his head.

The day Kizzie was playing jacks with Cocoa. Miss Nellie had had chores for him to do so it was later than usual by the time he arrived. Miss Mazie was inside visiting with Miss Lizzie.

Kizzie and Cocoa were sitting on the porch with the jacks, entertaining themselves. He had pedaled as fast as he could to get there and was out of breath.

He slid to a stop at the bottom of the steps, laid his bike on its side and went up to sit on the fourth step. He was now in the middle of the trio, one step down, Kizzie on his left, Cocoa on the right. Kizzie, after greeting him "show off", introduced her friend in the way of a six year old.

"This Cocoa."

"Hi" said Zak. "How come your hair is white?"

Kizzie immediately clamped both hands over her mouth and mumbled "Uh Oh."

Cocoa made a small fist with her right hand and let go with all the force her little four year old arms could muster, right upside Zak's curly topped head.

He didn't know if it was the force of the punch or his sheer surprise at not seeing it coming that sent him sprawling to land at the end of the stairs.

Without a word Cocoa pushed the jacks over to Kizzie and pranced off into the house.

"She don't like people to talk about her hair," she defended her friend.

Zak rose slowly, brushing dirt that didn't exist from his clothes, hoping to God the humiliation he felt at being slugged by a four year old wasn't showing on his face.

"Geez, I wasn't talking 'bout her hair. I was just asking how come it was white."

"You just have to say you're sorry, then she'll be alright." Kizzie the mediator, even then.

Zak did as he was told.

From then on, it was him who was first to tackle anyone who mentioned Cocoa's hair, provided she didn't get to them first.

Zak let the thought fade as he focused his attention back to Kizzie. She was still sleeping, even, measured breaths which indicated she was in a deep sleep. It really must have been a long day and a half for her.

It would have taken being hog tied and strapped down for the Kizzie he had known to be caught taking a nap during the day. She had not been one to want to miss anything.

But she hadn't stirred since he came in, except to let the book drop from her hands to lay open on the table. He couldn't begin to imagine all that was on her mind but none of it was showing on her face. Her look was peaceful and he didn't have the heart to wake her.

He eased himself up off his knees and turned the chair so that he was sitting a position similar to hers, except his legs were stretched out lengthwise along the table and his arms folded across his chest.

Turning his head so he could watch her, he let his thoughts wander to their childhood again.

Chapter 13

Back then Zak had thought that part of Kizzie's attraction to him was because she had no brothers. Whereas Cocoa had been raised amid a slew of male cousins and extended family, Kizzie had no other immediate family in the area.

Both she and Cocoa were now their parent's only children but it had not always been that way.

Kizzie had an older brother who died when she wasn't quite three years old.

Zak had learned the story from Miss Nellie when he got older. The Carpenter's had a son, already nine years old by the time Kizzie was born.

His name was Dallas Jr. but his nickname was Spuggin.

The way Miss Nellie told it, Spuggin had adored his little sister and he was her idol. She had been late learning to walk because Spuggin carried her everywhere from the time she was in diapers.

He had a beautiful voice and according to Miss Nellie, sang incessantly to Kizzie no matter what he was doing. He would sit Kizzie down somewhere near him, whether it was chopping wood, feeding the chickens or toting water for Miss Lizzie's wash tubs. He wouldn't let her out of his sight.

He could be seen with Kizzie sitting straddled on his back, her little arms holding him tightly around the neck and his arms looped around the bend in each of her legs, running like the wind. Kizzie's laughter, and his, could be heard long before he got where he was going.

Miss Nellie told him that Spuggin got many a whipping for running with that child on his back. Miss Lizzie just knew he was going to fall one day and break both their necks.

The next chance he got, he'd do it again.

One of Spuggin's chores was to keep the fire going in the woodstove in the kitchen. The stove had a reservoir on the side that kept water heated for Miss Lizzie on wash day.

It was also used for filling the wash tubs for baths. Underneath the reservoir Mr. Dallas kept a small can of kerosene on the floor beside Miss Lizzie's grease can.

The story, according to Miss Nellie, was that when Spuggin was twelve and Kizzie not quite three, Miss Lizzie had made Spuggin put Kizzie down on the bed so that he could build up the fire in the stove.

What he would normally do was add more wood to the fire then pour a little bit of the grease on top of it to get it burning really hot.

This day, by mistake, he picked up the can of kerosene. The whole cookstove was in flames within seconds.

Miss Lizzie was scrubbing clothes on the washboard on the back porch and Mr. Dallas was in the back of the house, shucking corn.

They both had come running when they heard his screams. It was already too late. When they reached him, his hair, shirt, pants, everything was in a blaze.

According to Miss Nellie, Miss Lizzie told her that with all the pain that boy must have been in and as scared as he must have been, he was running toward the bedroom to where his baby sister was while they were trying to rip off his clothes.

They managed to get him outside and onto the ground but as cheap as his old shirt was, Miss Lizzie could not rip the buttons off that shirt. In the hospital, they did grafs using skin from Mr. Dallas but it was no use.

He lived for eight days, never regaining consciousness. The day they buried her, Miss Lizzie had the burn scars still on her hands.

Kizzie had wakened when she heard Spuggin's screams.

Miss Lizzie said she was standing at the foot of the bed with her arms outstretched to her brother; piercing screams so loud it was hard to believe they were coming out of a baby that small.

Her little face soaked with tears. It had taken Miss Lizzie, with her hands bandaged, and Mr. Dallas, their own tears and heartache mixed with their daughter's, hours just holding her and rocking her, back and forth, back and forth, to finally calm her down.

For weeks afterwards she had nightmares each time she went to sleep.

Then suddenly one day, the nightmares were gone, the crying stopped and she was acting like a normal three year old. It was like she had put the whole thing away in her mind where she didn't have to deal with it.

To their knowledge she hadn't said a word about it since. Zak never mentioned to her that he knew the story.

Zak came to himself and realized he had tears on his face. He cried for her now as he had cried when Miss Nellie first told him the story. It was incomprehensible to him why anyone, especially a little baby, would have to see such a thing.

With both hands he wiped his face, then ran his hands down the front of his uniform. He looked at his watch. As bad as he hated to do it, he was going to have to wake her.

Cocoa had sent him to fetch her and she would have his hide if he got back late. He remembered how that fist had felt when she was four years old. He had no desire to take one on from her now.

Leaning across the table he traced her dried tears. She stirred. Very gently he pinched the end of her nose. This time she came fully awake, opening her eyes but not moving from her position.

After the few seconds it took for her to get her bearings, she became aware of Zak sitting across from her, in uniform.

"Hey," from him.

"Hey," from her.

"Hey doll."

"Hey you."

She continued.

"What now, Sheriff? You planning to arrest me for fraternizing with the Old Lady Who Lived in a Shoe?"

"Well now, that surely is an interesting proposition, seeing as how I'd have to strip search you for weapons and all."

She rolled her eyes! "Being an officer of the law, it's my sworn duty to look out for the town's safety."

She rolled them again. "However, right now, one Miss Sullivan...", he didn't get to finish.

"Oh my God. The luncheon! What time is it? And Solomon and Burke were supposed to come by to help...And oh my God! I haven't even gotten dressed yet! How long have I been asleep? Why didn't you wake me?"

Kizzie had already popped up from the chair and was halfway through the door when Zak caught up to her.

Like they said...she could sum up a situation and have a plan before most folks even had a grasp on what was going on.

He reached out and grabbed her elbow from behind.

"Hey! Hey! Wait a minute. Slow down! I don't know how many questions were in there but let me take a shot.

The time...it's about nine thirty. Solomon and Burke drove up about the same time I did. I showed them where to put your stuff. They moved everything in and they're already gone. You have plenty of time to get dressed. I don't know how long you were sleeping before I got here but I've been here about a half an hour. I didn't wake you because you looked so beautiful sleeping I was just sitting there making my eyes happy.

So, did I cover everything? Feeling better?"

"Actually yes, I do." She said, feeling a little foolish. "Guess I got a little panicky. I had no intention of going to sleep. When you mentioned Cocoa it reminded me that she said she would be back for me around eleven and I hate to ever be late."

Zak followed her as she left the center and made her way back across the driveway. As they entered the screened front porch Zak told her, "Yeah, I remember that about you.

But since it will only take us about ten minutes to drive to the park, there was no point in waking you sooner. You looked so peaceful, I hated to wake you up when I did."

The 'us' was not lost on Kizzie.

"You mean I'm riding with you to the park?"

"Fraid so my dear lady. Seems like the Ladies Auxiliary thought it only decent and proper that the town's most noted dignitary be given an official escort by the town's sheriff.

I couldn't agree more. I am honored to be at your service." Zak took a bow. "Listen Kiz, I didn't mean to upset you last night..."

"It's ok. No harm done. And I didn't mean to go off like that. I don't know where it came from." He bowed again.

Kizzie sighed. There just was no hope for him. She noticed again that he was in full dress uniform. She also couldn't help but notice that every fold fit his well toned body like it was custom made.

"Now, he continued, I don't know if the good ladies are as much interested in your dignitary status as they are at shining the spotlight on themselves but it sure will be fun to play along, don't you think?"

What else could she do? She meant what she had told herself earlier about making a stronger effort to be more gracious and appreciative.

There could be worse things than putting up with Zak's teasing.

He had been talking as they walked. They followed the wrap around, the opposite side from the direction Kizzie took when she came out and were now at the glassed in porch. Kizzie went first through the narrow set of French doors.

"Well, I'm afraid I'll have to ask you to wait while I get dressed. Would you like something to drink?"

"Matter of fact I would, it's warm out already. But I'll get it myself. You go ahead and get started. Take your time."

"Ok then. I'll be down in a half hour." She backed her way out through the kitchen, wondering why on earth she was feeling so nervous. She started upstairs.

He yelled to her back "Can I watch?" All he heard was mumbling he was sure were words even he wouldn't repeat. He laughed to himself as he hit the kitchen in search of anything cold. What she actually said was "that's why I'm nervous."

Chapter 14

Hillside Park was just a few miles East of town.

Instead of the ten minutes Zak had promised, the ride took more than an hour. Instead of taking the service road that ran parallel to the main highway, Zak had chosen to drive right through the middle of Main Street.

This route took them past the old elementary school. He pulled the car near the abandoned playground and stopped.

"Did you know they built a new school? There's just the one for all grades still but it's a lot bigger."

Kizzie wondered why he had stopped but decided not to ask. "Uhm huh, Cocoa told me."

"I'm glad you two have stayed close all these years." Still Kizzie said nothing.

Zak got out and came around to open the door for Kizzie. "Let's walk for a minute."

He led her by the hand over to the old seasaw. Most of the wood had rotted so they couldn't rock like they used to. He offered her a seat on the round wood pole that supported the saw.

"Things have been moving so fast since you got here, we haven't had a chance to talk."

"I'm not sure we have that much to talk about." Kizzie kept her eyes lowered, her feet crossed at the ankles, not quite reaching the ground.

"Well, maybe I just feel like I need to talk to you. But today probably is not the best time to say most of what I'd like to, what I need to, say. So much time has already passed us by and I don't want to lose anymore.

Back there watching you sleep, I felt just the way I used to, as though nothing had changed. I could have sat there for hours and just looked at you. I know I don't have the right to spring this on you now. I know I hurt you. Badly. I would give both my legs if I could change it. I can't. But I would like to try to make it up to you. I just want you to promise me you'll give me a chance to try to explain before you head back home."

"Look at me Kizzie. Please."

She raised her head to look at him.

"I don't blame you for being angry. You have every right. I just want the chance to try to explain. I think it will help you resolve some things, especially with you and Seal. Come on. You owe me that much, at least, right? Besides, there's not even a toll."

"What does she have to do with this?"

"That's not exactly the question I'd hoped you'd answer first." Zak said, feigning disappointment."

Giving in, knowing this was not the battle he needed to choose right now, he told her.

"You'll know after we talk. Promise me Kiz?"

"Actually, I don't know if I'm going back home right away. You did hurt me Zak. I've carried it around with me for twenty five years." She sounded very tired. "Maybe it is time to let it all go. When do you want us to talk?"

"Tomorrow night!. How about I take you out... maybe over to Stoney's? You know the whole town is just waiting to see how long it'll take for us to be seen together?"

"That sounds like it might be nice. Actually."

"Good. Good. First though, I need to know something."

Kizzie looked at him as if to say he was really pushing it.

"I just have to know. How in hell's name did you pull this off? You know how the people round here talk. I've heard ten different versions of that story but you can't believe any of 'em. Some people have part of the facts; some people have none so they make up whatever suits 'em and then you've got those who take parts of both versions and make up still another story. And pulling shit out of Cocoa was like taking Jack Daniel away from my mother!"

"Zak!!"

"Well it's true."

That was her Zak "We got time?"

"We've got time."

It only took her about twenty minutes to tell him the story.

"Actually, it was more about having a good memory and liking puzzles than it was about having a plan.

You know how messed up I was after my folks drowned."

His thoughtful look caused her to pause. They both remembered.

He knew just how messed up she had been. It was in May and the weather was still cool. The day of the funeral she had finally come out of that closet.

After the funeral when everyone was back at the house she had stood for a long time looking out the front screen door. As the days got warmer, the screens would be taken out of the attic to replace all the panes of glass. At the moment the panes were still inset.

His heart was breaking as much as hers as he watched her.

Without warning, she raised her right fist and did a right jab on the glass panel. Cocoa had walked up just in time for a piece of shattered glass to slice through her wrist. Kizzie had crumbled in a little ball on the floor.

The three of them sat there, huddled and crying, arms around each other, Cocoa refusing to leave her friend to get her arm tended.

The house had been filled to the roof with friends of the Carpenters.

After Kizzie's collapse Miss Mazie, the twins, Seal, Cocoa and Zak had taken turns making sure she was never alone for a minute.

Like Cocoa, Zak felt completely helpless. He watched her go through the motions, thanking everyone, serving food, being gracious the way Miss Lizzie would have expected.

He wished they all would leave.

Finally, the only ones left were Miss Mazie and Cocoa. Kizzie insisted they take the rest of the food. She wasn't sure if she would ever again have an appetite.

Miss Mazie wrapped her arms around Kizzie one more time, knowing she could never fill the void left by her best friend.

But she prayed fervently that God would give her the strength to be there for her, and to give strength to Kizzie. "Bless this child Lord! Not just today but a long time to come."

When they were finally gone, Kizzie stood in the middle of the living room. Zak had never seen anyone look so alone and lost. If he could have seen his own face, he would recognize the same look mirrored back at him.

To add to his sadness, he carried his own separate burden of guilt and shame.

After what seemed like hours, he walked to where she was and taking her hand, led her like a hapless child over to the sofa.

"Look at me Kiz."

She was only seventeen, he nineteen. He had no earthly idea what he could say to her to ease her pain, convince her that it would be ok.

"Look at me Kiz, he repeated, more forcefully, using his thumb and forefinger to lift her chin.

"It's not real, is it Zak?" Please tell me this isn't real. They can't both be gone. They can't both be gone. What am I going to do without Mama? What am I going to do?"

She couldn't hold back the flood. He felt even more helpless.

Not knowing what else to do he pulled her closer to him. He kissed her tears. He used his shirt sleeve to wipe her nose. He whispered softly to her. "I wish I had answers for you Precious. Maybe one day it will make some sense. I do know this. I will be here for you. Always. You never have to worry or be afraid. We'll do this together, you and me."

He rocked her there on the couch, wrapping himself around her like a cocoon. His shirt was wet from her tears. He never noticed.

He caressed her back as he held her. Neither of them could have seen it coming but this intimate sharing of pain would ignite a fire that Time could not extinguish.

Zak could feel his need for her begin a slow burn. He was determined to ignore it. Fate would remind him that it was out of his hands.

She could feel his steady heartbeat grow stronger with every beat. She held onto him tighter.

Her Pop Pop Dallas and Mama were gone. In one day! In one moment! How was that possible? Her

Mama had just given her that wonderful hug and kiss that morning and told her what a good girl she was to help her with all the housework then go over and help Miss Mazie with her windows. "You just keep doing the right thing Child. God will bless you. Yes he will, she'd said.

Pop Pop Dallas had lifted her two feet into the air with that bear hug of his. In his quiet way he told her the same, except he actually said "Squirt" and pulled her plaits after he'd sat her back down. Then they had left to go fishing. Pop Pop Dallas said he was going to catch a mess of fresh perch or some catfish for supper.

They never came home!

But Zak was here as he had been since she could remember. He made her feel less scared.

Suddenly she felt a heat in the crossroad of her thighs so intense she almost giggled out loud. That would be all she'd need. To have Zak get his hands on that little bit of information and not only would he think he did have a real maniac on his hands but he would laugh at her too.

Kizzie was about to learn her first big girl lesson. Some things can't be wished away.

The heat stayed. Another ember started in her belly and moved its way up to settle in her breasts, already swollen and full. If she had shackled it with a thousand irons, she could not have slowed its journey.

To the contrary, every time she felt his heart beat, hers answered in return.

"Love me Zak. Please." It was not a demand nor a plea but a yearning heart, reaching out for the only love left in her life. First Spuggin was gone and now her folks.

He answered her by taking her hand. He led her around the corner of the living room and up the one and a half flight stairway. He opened the door to a room he had practically grown up in. Yet for a split second, he felt like an intruder.

She let him lead her to the iron bed, slightly larger than a twin, that he had slept in as much as she. This time would be unlike any from before. This time they would cross a threshold which had no reverse.

He helped her with buttons on the back of her dress, as he had done countless times before.

"Zak, come help me with my buttons. Mama can't hear me", she'd yell from this same bedroom window.

"Coming Master."

"Yeah, yeah. Just come help me."

"Hey, I like your back."

"You're asking for it Zak Bishop. I'm gonna have to hit you!"

"You promise!

When the two bodies touched, it was like fanning flames in a fireplace. Zak traced the line of heat with his lips from her eyes to her toenails then back up on the other side.

On the way he parked at her naval, just long enough to make a circle of tiny kisses around it. His mouth followed the trail to her breasts. They were warm and soft.

He made another pit stop, letting his cheeks rest between her breasts. He turned his head to take one nipple, then the other.

She lifted her head to meet his kiss as his journey continued upward. The contact was electric. Sparks spread through her veins that reminded her of embers flying upward in a fireplace when the burning wood got stoked.

There were no words to describe what Zak felt.

He released her lips to speak gently into her ear.

"Listen to me love. You don't ever have to be afraid of me Precious. I would die before I would hurt you or let anyone else hurt you. You believe me?

She only possessed enough strength to nod slowly, her eyes never leaving his face.

"Then please, please trust me Precious. I've loved you from the first moment I saw you. I love you now. Trust me baby!"

She did.

It was sometime later that Zak had kissed her eyelids, her nose, each cheek and then her mouth.

She was groggy.

"What time is it" How long was I asleep?"

"Only a little while." He told her softly "Kiz, you trust me right? She nodded. "Then there's something I need for you to do for me."

Neither one of them was ready for a family. He remembered Candy's lessons.

Candy was the prostitute his father had 'given him' for his twelfth birthday. She had taught him everything he needed to know about the art of lovemaking.

She sat in the tub of hot soapy water while he bathed her like a child. He rubbed every part until she was dry then dropped her gown over her head. She made no sound. He led her back to the bedroom and tucked her in between clean cool sheets.

"Get some rest Precious. We'll be ok, you and me". He turned off the light in the bedroom and lay down in his usual spot on the floor. Just in case she needed him.

It had been several days. Zak and Cocoa were worried about her. Nothing he or anyone did, not even Cocoa, seemed to lift her spirits. Cocoa looked to Miss Mazie. "Just love her Child and pray. Pray for her Child." Even so, Kizzie wasn't herself. After the funerals she didn't seem to have any life left. She went on that way for months.

By the time she finished out that last year of high school, he could see some of the old Kizzie. That's when he had added to her heartbreak.

Kizzie shook off the memory then went on with her story.

"I didn't know what to do with myself. Even after Miss Mazie made me leave the house and come live with her, it wasn't the same, even being there with Cocoa.

Then you left the next year and I was really lost. I don't even know what I did for the next two years.

When I was almost nineteen this lawyer shows up out of the blue. He tells me, Miss Mazie and Big Jake that I had this huge sum of money coming from my folks' life insurance. He said it took so long because there had been an investigation. I guess because both of them died at the same time the insurance company wanted to make sure it hadn't been some crazy double suicide or some other kind of dumb shit. He said something about double indemnity.

I've learned since then what that meant but at the time he was telling us I didn't have a clue; and didn't care. I just wanted my mother and father back.

Anyway, the money had been held in an estate so I had a nice tidy sum of over two hundred thousand dollars. Can you believe it!!!I was of legal age then so I could claim it whenever I wanted. I couldn't even think numbers that high.

I didn't think about it at all for more than a year afterwards.

By the time our twentieth birthday rolled around, I was suffocating. I was pretty sure by then you weren't coming back so there was very little to hold me here.

I offered Miss Mazie and Big Jake some of the money but they wouldn't take it.

So I went to the bank and took sixty thousand dollars out, in cash! Had the rest transferred here to Mr. Grady's bank. Had to drive all the way in to Rawlins.

The bank clerk almost messed in his drawers when I told him his bank was gonna have to give up that much money.

I came back, gave Cocoa fifty thousand and made her promise not to mention it to anybody. You should've seen us. We were in that closet for hours, counting and recounting that money! There's probably still a couple hundred dollar bills in there."

"Let's go," Zak pretended to take off. He got a little bit of the smile he was trying for.

She ignored him.

"I had seen this ad for a secretary for a land management company in New Beaumont, a small town outside of Hartford, Connecticut. I had taken typing in high school so I knew I could do well at it if I got the job. I did.

I took more classes and got a two year business certificate. I started to move up.

One of my assignments was doing research for commercial real estate companies. It was field work supporting the facts supplied by the title companies. It was fun and I enjoyed it because it involved a lot of travel.

I was a quick study, I loved the details, fact-finding and putting it all together; like a puzzle. My boss respected how hard I worked to be so young. He took a genuine interest in helping me. He made sure I learned every detail about the business.

The one thing he always used to tell me was that the devil was in the details. "Don't dismiss any little detail, Miss Carpenter, no matter how insignificant you think it might be." I'll always be grateful to him for that because that's how I found out how to stop what was going on here.

Oddly enough, one of the research projects he gave me was for a company, Capstone, trying to buy property over in Clement. The deal had been axed but I didn't remember that little detail until I started looking into Smithville.

I had been there for five years when I got a job offer from one of the associate companies in Vista, Arizona.

The company was in the same industry but my job was as an assistant to the marketing director. It offered a good relocation package and a chance to have more creative input into my work. I took it and I've lived there since.

My boss, Jill was a tough woman. She put together some deals that still make my head spin. She was working on an ad campaign for this jeans company that wanted to expand.

Guess what they wanted to expand into...Cotton tee shirts and one hundred percent cotton sheets. Anyway, with the upstart charges and the cost of the branding campaign, the investors kept pushing it back.

They thought risking that kind of money on a new product line didn't make sound business sense. Jill was determined to pull off the deal. She convinced the CEO of the jeans company to agree to take the deal back to the investors if she could find a way to cut a million dollars out of their investment commitment. She had no idea how she was going to do it.

She was still wrestling with putting it together when I came home to visit Cocoa five years ago.

While I was here I heard the talk about all the land being bought up by this company that wanted to build the new highway. I was too upset by what went down while I was here to think much about it.

But when I got back and Jill was still working on the deal, I remembered Cocoa telling me about what had happened in Clement and everyone being afraid the same thing was going to happen here.

A light bulb went off and after I thought it through it made perfect sense. I didn't mention it, even to Cocoa until I was sure it could work.

In order for us to cut a million dollars several things would have to happen; number one, we would have to almost get the land for free; number two, the new location for the factory would have to be located near the raw materials, otherwise what was saved on the land would be eaten up by transportation costs and number three, the tax base could not be inhibitive.

What better place than right here in Smithville! If the farmers were going to have to lose their land why not negotiate a sale that would be great for the town instead of being forced to sell it and have nothing to show for it.

That's when I remembered my old boss and the details. If the original company, Capstone, that wanted the land in Smithville had fought so hard to get it, they obviously thought it was prime real estate.

They didn't back off from trying to buy it without a very good reason. So how was it that this current company, Harriman Developers, was able to buy the land in Clement and the adjacent property here in Smithville without even so much as a by your leave.

That's what I was determined to find out. I had to know that one detail before I could take the proposal to Jill. She would have to sell it to the investors who would have to sell it to the Smithville council. I was so excited I couldn't sleep for days. To make a long story short…"

The teasing look on his face said it was way too late for that, but she knew he wanted to hear the rest. She dared him to utter a sound, "you asked for this story, now you're going to hear it.'

After a minute, he waved his hands in a scooped bow.

"Please continue Miss Carpenter," using the tone she'd used for her old boss.

"Anyway…I tracked down one of the researchers at my old company. All he could tell me was Capstone's deal fell flat because of their government contractor status. And something about land grants. That didn't make sense because companies like that make most of their money off of those type contracts. What the heck was up with this one?

As it turns out, a great deal of farm land in and around Smithville had been 'deeded' in the form of land grants to certain individuals during the civil war. These families had worked the farms for a number of years; therefore making it their only means of support.

Zak was interested. "Sort of like squatters' rights?"

"Exactly," Zizzie went on.

Once deeded, the government cannot reclaim that land as long as there is at least one living direct descendent of the original grantee. If no direct descendents can be located within the timeframe established by the land office, then the property reverts back to the state.

But, even if the government legally reclaims the land, it cannot pay a contractor to develop a structure, in this case the highway, if they, the government, also sold them the land on which it would be built. It's called double dipping in the taxpayer's pocket."

"Wait, let me make sure I got this straight. Harriman paid the state money for the land, now the state is going to give it right back to them to build the highway."

"There you go. It was perfectly legal for the state to sell the land to Harriman. But by also giving them the highway contract directly, the state denied other firms the opportunity to bid. It failed its fiduciary duty to support the growth of small businesses.

Not exactly a charge your elected officials are likely to get excited about."

"Well, I'll be damned."

"My thoughts exactly." Kizzie concurred.

"Capstone got wind of this land grant and did the smart thing. Instead of dedicating hundreds of resources and who knows how much money trying to find out first if there was a grant still in existence, then second trying to negotiate a deal, he withdrew his offer to the state in the time frame allotted by law. That way he lost nothing except the time spent putting the deal together in the first place.

Harriman, however, is up shit creek without a paddle because they either didn't find out about the grant before they made the bid, or they did know about it and decided to roll the dice, gambling that no one else would."

Zak really was intrigued by her story. "So what did you do?"

"I found the land grant!" They both beamed.

"It took some doing but I had the advantage of being born and raised in this town. And the blessings of parents who knew everybody who ever lived here. They used to tell us those old stories, remember?

It had only been a little over a hundred years since the civil war. Most of the people still living here are in their seventies or older. That's just one generation away...that grant could have been owned by a grandfather or a grandmother of someone I knew.

So I poured through hundreds of documents at the State Land Office. Without a name to begin with, it meant I would have to search every grant deeded in this part of the state.

I practically lived there for weeks. But I had this feeling I couldn't shake and I had to keep believing and keep trying. Then one day, wham, there it was!

The grant described the exact boundaries for twenty five hundred acres, east, west, north and south, plus the adjacent properties. It listed the deed holders from 1869 to the present. It was fascinating stuff to read. The last entry conveyed the property to one Miss Eddie Jean Burlock in 1910, mother of our one and only...

"Miss Eddie?" You've gotta be kidding me!"

"Nope, the portrait lady herself. So Jill and I set up a meeting with the Harriman office. She explained to them, in the very nice way she has about her, that they had purchased fifteen hundred acres of real property the state had no legal right to sell; that they had made an offer to buy the remaining thousand acres and that they were able to buy that property by withholding certain information from the state.

She further explained that she was obligated to make this information available to her client and should she do so, the Harrimans would be tied up in lawsuits well into the next century. However, if they chose to withdraw any and all pending offers within a fifty mile radius of Smithville she might see her way clear to letting this information remain in her files.

They hemmed and hawed about it but she held their feet to the fire. The woman had guts.

"The rest you know already. Miss Eddie sold the property to the town for one dollar; you know they offered her a substantial share but she never would accept it? You know what she asked for?"

"Let me guess. Permission to have her portrait put up on those three mile markers outside of town."

"Hey, you're pretty quick for an old man. At her age she wasn't interested in money. That portrait represented respect for Miss Eddie and everyone who saw it would have to acknowledge it, grudgingly or not.

"The council negotiated a deal to lease the property for twenty years and the company agreed to hire first from Smithville and Clement. The money from the lease and the influx of jobs will be enough to change the economic outlook of this entire county for the next few decades."

"My Kizzie, the super sleuth. Seriously, we all have a lot to thank you for Kiz. I am so damn proud of you." He wanted to hug her but thought he'd better not push his luck too far too soon. "But hey, we'd better get going."

Her shoes had fallen to the ground as she was swinging her legs. He scooped them up first, then reached down and scooped her up as easily as he did the shoes.

"Zak!!! "Oh hell, thought Kizzie. Just enjoy the ride."

In spite of herself Kizzie *had* started to feel like a celebrity, of sorts.

Back in the car, it was only minutes before they were in the middle of Main Street, crawling at a snail's pace. Even though most of the shops were closed and just about everyone already at the park or headed that way, there were a number of people still on the street.

When Zak had driven past the House of Hair, there was a huge sign hanging from the awning which read-Closed for the Holiday. The parking spaces in front of the shop, normally full on a Saturday, were all empty.

A few children on bicycles caught up to Zak's police car and rode alongside, waving and whistling at Kizzie. Zak blew the horn in several short bursts to acknowledge the waves.

Several people were coming out of Mr. Young's grocery, loaded down with last minute items needed at the picnic.

They maneuvered their bags into one arm so they could wave at her and shout Welcome Home Kizzie. She waved back, yelling Thank You while Zak continued to blow the horn.

Last out of the store was Mr. Young. His head was covered with a close cut crop of salt and pepper hair. He was dressed nicely in dark khakis and a white short sleeved pullover. He must be well over seventy by now but except for a slight bend in his back, he looked healthy and strong.

He waved Kizzie a welcome home, closing the door and adding his own sign that read- Closed for the Holiday.

The greetings continued all along Main Street, people waving and Zak laying on his horn much more than she thought necessary.

But she had committed to join in the fun so she continued to wave while Zak filled in names for faces she vaguely remembered.

At Jessie White's filling station they saw Solomon and Burke, dumping several large bags of ice into the largest ice chest she'd ever seen, wedged into the bed of a pickup. She was sure it would be filled with beer, sodas, jars of lemonade and God only knew what else.

The party was on!

"Hello Kizzie...from Solomon!!

"Welcome home Kizzie...from Burke.

She waved until they were out of sight.

"Did either of those two ever get married?" Kizzie asked. Oddly enough, after telling him the story earlier, she felt more at ease with him now. Almost like old times.

"They both did, believe it or not. You remember they were raised by their grandmother, Miss Hattie Davis? She passed away a few years back.

They had done a lot of work on the house thanks to the business at the diner they owned. After she passed, they finished the house and went right on living in it."

Solomon and Burke Davis were identical twins. The only way to tell them apart was Solomon had a perfectly round mole the size of a pencil eraser flat against his skin on his left cheek.

They both had dimples so deep everyone called them pits. When Solomon smiled the mole would get lost in the pit.

Burke was the one who talked with his own version of the English language. Instead of pronouncing repeat, it was RE-peat, rewind was RE-wind, reward was RE-ward; home equity was ekkity and alzheimers was alltimers. It took some getting used to and Kizzie, being the lover of reading that she was growing up with them, used to bite down on her lip to stop herself from constantly correcting him.

Their mother had been very young and unmarried when she had gotten pregnant. Solomon Burke was an up and coming crooner of love ballads and their mother adored him.

The local story was that she played his records over and over, never tiring of hearing him sing. When the twins were born, she named them after her idol.

She left them with her mother when they were two and wasn't heard from since except to show up at her mother's funeral.

When she found out that anything her mother had of value had been left to her grandsons, she disappeared just as quickly as she had shown up.

The twins had formed a strong brotherly bond. They learned to take care of themselves and their grandmother.

Both loved to cook. Together the two of them opened the Fish Swamp, the only diner in town except for Miss Eddie's, which was more a strip bar than a restaurant.

They served fried catfish with cabbage and cornbread that any woman in town who thought she could cook would envy.

Zak was still telling her about them.

"They enrolled in business school over in Clement before Miss Hattie died.

They didn't have a car so they would borrow one from whoever could spare it at the time. They drove an hour each way twice a week for months.

I would take them whenever I could. They were determined to learn how to run a business, and they did. They met the women at the school they later married.

They both have kids; Solomon two girls and Burke two boys. No twins. But it's the oddest thing you ever saw. All four of them look just like Solomon and Burke.

Their mother will still come around every now and then just to take whatever money she can sweet talk from her sons, then she's gone again until the next time she needs money."

Zak finished what he was saying about the twins and pointed up ahead. They had reached the park. Zak stopped the car at the entrance. A large sign read ' Hillside Park – Proudly Maintained by Smithville's Department of Recreation'.

"Look."

Chapter 15

Kizzie looked past the sign. She couldn't believe what she was seeing. After the last two days she didn't think there were any surprises left. She was mistaken.

She opened the car door and stood on the frame.

The scene before her, an expansion of the lake they had fished and swam in as children was beautiful beyond anything she had thought this small, sleepy town could produce.

About twenty yards to her right was where the lake used to be. It had been drained and excavated. Where dark water once was there was now a huge pit filled with white sand.

She knew this was the same lake because the huge old oak, with roots as large as small trees, had been saved. The limbs stretched out so far that one of them held four swings made from chain link fencing and wood seats. The swings were still there, with newer seats. A volleyball net was set dead center.

At either end were gigantic sand boxes, some made of whitewashed wood and others from colorful heavy plastics.

A grill was set up at the end nearest Kizzie with a picnic table and benches anchored in cement. The area was filled with kids playing volleyball and hauling pails of sand to make sandcastles.

A blue checkered tablecloth covered the picnic table. On top of it were plates, cups, napkins, jars of mustard and ketchup, pickles and preserves; all it needed now was the hamburgers and hotdogs that would later be cooked on the grill.

To the left of the old lake, was a new man made lake the size of a football field, shaped like an hourglass.

Across the narrow middle, the prettiest pedestrian bridge Kizzie had ever seen ran from one side to the other. Each end rose out of the water about ten feet, supported on three foot round wooden poles.

The floor of the bridge was made from wide wooden planks, tuck and groove style so there were no open gaps. It was painted with the same whitewash stain as the picnic tables and wide enough for a car to drive across.

Midway, a pergola with cushioned benches had been erected on one side and a short pier on the other. Three or four boys had already cast their fishing rods from the pier for the catch of the day. Several people were crossing in each direction, headed for the opposite sides.

Around the perimeter of the new lake, a carpet of grass so green it looked artificial, was freshly mowed.

It would stand up against any of the professionally manicured golf courses where she lived in Vista.

"Cow manure." Zak knew what she was thinking.

"Oh Zak. I think it is the prettiest park I've ever seen."

"You haven't seen the best yet", he said, baiting her curiosity. He stayed quiet as she completed the visual tour.

Colorful blankets, towels and bedspreads dotted the lawn. Most were unoccupied, being held down with small coolers or lawn chairs to keep them from being blown away. One blanket was anchored with a pair of boots, laid in diagonal corners.

Zak explained that some of the forward thinking citizens were making sure they had the best seats in the house for fireworks later that night.

Large, ageless oak trees had been left intact, lining the outer rim of the grass. At the base of each tree was a wide circle of low growing colorful ground foliage. A different color had been planted around each tree and was meticulously manicured.

Kizzie was starting to understand the 'Proudly Maintained' phrase on the sign.

North of the bridge at the far end of the lake she saw what she thought was a huge area with three large covered tents. There were more picnic tables spread out in the areas outside the tents. Everyone seemed to be heading in that direction.

"Come on, get in. I think word's gotten out that the guest of honor has arrived."

The trees separated the lake area from the large parking lot on the east. The paved road followed the line of oaks past the filled parking lot. Kizzie saw no one directing traffic in the lot yet every car was evenly spaced and no one was hemmed in.

"I've died and gone to Norman Rockwell heaven."

Zak couldn't help but smile. That had been his exact reaction the first time he'd seen the finished product.

He didn't park the car with the others, instead choosing to follow the road to the top of the lake. People lined the road on both sides.

It was several yards from the lot to the tent area and the line looked ten deep all the way on both sides. When they saw the car approach, the applause began and grew louder as they got closer.

Zak blasted the siren but somehow Kizzie wasn't startled. Adults and children leaned in to touch her through the open window. As Zak drove past them, a procession formed alongside the car and a band behind it.

They arrived at the tents together, then moved away in order to give Zak room to pull into the designated parking space in back of the picnic tables.

Before Kizzie could open the door Zak called out. "Wait. I'll come get you." He jogged around to the passenger side, opening the door with a flourish.

"You're really making too much of this you know," giggling in spite of trying to take the whole thing seriously.

"Ladies and gentlemen – I give you- Miss Kizzie Carpenter."

At that exact moment someone pulled the lever on a machine not visible from the car. All Kizzie could see were millions of tiny bubbles as they floated in a hundred different directions, mixing in with the crowd as though they also belonged. Kizzie giggled as she held out both hands to see how many she could catch.

The applause and screams were deafening. He led her through the crowd to the head table, set for ten.

Miss Mazie, Seal, Mr. Young, Mayor Dennis and Solomon and Burke were already seated. The remaining seats were designated for Kizzie at the center, Zak, Cocoa and Thomas.

The table in the tent next to them was also set for ten. A large placard announced that it was reserved for the Ladies of the Auxiliary, who were slowly drifting toward their seats.

The remaining tent had a table of twelve already seated. Kizzie recognized Mr. Grady, Miss Eddie, Miss Gertie, Mr.Tanner, Mr. Bloom and Jessie White. Mrs. Tanner was there but had refused to sit near her husband, taking the seat farthest from him.

They waved to her again and she smiled back. She couldn't recall the names of the others.

Kizzie looked around for Cocoa and found her talking with Thomas, busy setting up the sound stage with large speakers and stereo equipment. A tablecloth draped over the equipment table advertised 'Dee Jay Tommy B'.

Tommy B had it going on tonight. He was decked out in chocolate brown pleated trousers. His lighter brown dress shirt was hanging on a nail near his setup.

"Would you check out this arrogance!! Cocoa waved her over. She was pointing to Thomas' chest. "Do you believe this man? You know he ain't talking about no bananas."

Kizzie read Thomas' shirt. It was a white, sleeveless t-shirt. Two cartoon monkeys were on the front. Each one was holding a banana. One-somewhat larger than the other, monkey and banana. Written underneath was 'Mine's Bigger'.

Kizzie laughed again for the umpteenth time that day. "You gotta love the confidence Cocoa!"

Just then Zak arrived to show her to her seat. He pulled out the chair designated for her at the center of the table and Kizzie sat.

Looking around she was glad she had changed her mind about wearing the shorts she had originally thought about. Mother Nature delivered on the promise of good weather.

The sun was warm but not hot and a slight breeze moved through the tents. No one was wearing their finest but they had certainly stepped up the dress code a notch. Most of the men were dressed similar to Mr. Young.

The women all wore pretty sundresses or skirts and sleeveless tops. Every woman of the auxiliary was wearing some type of hat, in the true tradition of real southern women.

Kizzie's sundress was buttery yellow with a darker shade of yellow lace piping around the edges of the bodice. Thin spaghetti straps held up the bodice which criss-crossed her breasts, falling in soft ruffles and shaping a low vee without showing too much cleavage.

The skirt, in soft georgette cotton gathered with hundreds of tiny folds at the dropped waistline, lay nicely across the top of her hips. The billowy folds stopped about midway her calves. She wore matching hi heeled yellow sandals with tiny straps across the toes set off by tiny gold buckles.

It was too hot for earrings and necklaces so her only jewelry was a row of twenty thin gold bangles on her right arm from wrist to elbow.

Zak stood behind her for a few moments after she was seated. He leaned down to put his head close to her ear. "Did I tell you how lovely you look today?"

She shook her head no.

"Well, take my gun and shoot me, cause I am definitely derelict in my duty."

"If I had one right now I probably would shoot you," she laughed.

"Speaking of duty, I've got some things to take care of back in town. I'll be back later. Save me a seat?"

She pat the seat of the chair beside her. He pinched her cheek and turned to leave. As he did so she noticed Seal get up and follow him as he walked to his car.

She couldn't hear what they were saying but the conversation didn't look friendly. Seal touched Zak's arm as though she was trying to change his mind about something. He shook her off and got in his car.

Just the sight of Seal was making her blood boil. She was trying hard to keep her temper under control. It was getting harder by the minute.

Cocoa arrived just as Zak drove off. Kizzie stood up to face her.

"Why is she here, Cocoa?"

"What! No hello Cocoa, it's been hours since I saw you. I miss you. I love you. No hugs for your best friend?"

"You know what I mean."

"You look gorgeous. I love your outfit."

Cocoa, you know how I feel about her. This is not funny."

"Yes, Kizzie. I do know what you mean," Cocoa started, dropping all pretense of keeping Kizzie off the subject of Seal. "She wants to be here. It wouldn't have been right to tell her she couldn't come. Especially when the rest of the entire county is here."

"It wasn't everybody who did what she did. You know that and you still think its ok for her to be here. And to sit her at the same table? I can't believe you would do that to me."

"You don't know the whole story Kiz. It wasn't like you think. You're just too damned stubborn to stop hating her long enough to find out the truth. She was our friend too, back then. You need to give her a chance."

"I know enough of the truth. I know my parents aren't here and it's her fault. I know that Zak stood me up the one time I needed him the most and on the same night the last person who saw him before he left town was her. That's all the truth I need to know."

Seal was back at the table. She stood at her chair at the end of the row across from Kizzie. She half smiled as she met Kizzie's gaze.

"Welcome home Kizzie. I didn't get a chance to tell you yesterday. It's good to have you back."

Miss Bessie Young, wife of Mr. Young, was talking loudly into the mike. The podium the mayor had used yesterday had been brought over and set up in the center of the three tents.

"Would everyone please take their seats? It's time to get started." It was clear that she took her job as president of the auxiliary seriously and was used to having her dictates obeyed. But it still took a few minutes to get everyone settled in their seats and quiet.

The excitement in the air was palpable and hard to contain.

Kizzie sat again without verbal acknowledgement to Seal. Seal looked at Cocoa and shrugged her shoulders. Cocoa could see the hurt but knew nothing more could be done at the moment.

"Welcome everyone. Welcome. Welcome. First, let us bow our heads while Reverend Newhouse leads us in our blessing. Reverend, would you do us the honor of blessing our tables?"

Reverend Newhouse said grace over the food, thanking God for the wonderful abundance, the wonderful women who prepared it, for sending the wonderful weather and for the wonderful folk who turned out today to welcome home one of their own. He stopped short of thanking Him for wonderful Kizzie, for fear of stealing any of Miss Bessie's thunder.

He took his seat. The only male at the table reserved for the Ladies Auxiliary. (Zak would have a comment about that Kizzie was sure).

"Thank you Reverend."

She cleared her throat, taking a minute to collect her thoughts. She had worked many hours on her short speech and seemed determined to do her club and herself proud with its oratory.

"Five years ago this town was dying. Three of the largest farms, almost fifteen hundred acres had been taken over and sold by the state to make way for the new highway. The loss of those farms put a lot of our men folk out of work.

The highway rerouted tourist traffic and people traveling on vacations right past Smithville which put even a greater strain on our local businesses. How in the world could we expect to survive when our economic base was being drug out from under us. Our young people were leaving as soon as they turned legal, a lot of them before, because we didn't have services to attract them to stay.

We all were hurting, trying to keep our businesses and the town from drowning in red ink. Then we found out some company was buying up land over in Clement and planned to buy another thousand acres here in Smithville.

If the State's plan to extend the highway the rest of the way to Clement had succeeded there's no way any of us would have survived. Smithville would have become a ghost town in months."

Not a sound could be heard anywhere in the crowd as Miss Bessie delivered this first part of her speech.

Kizzie could see why she had been chosen as their spokesman.

She spoke with conviction and passion, flailing her hands and marching back and forth to emphasize certain points.

Her mention of the freeway stirred feelings of anger still bubbling at the surface of nearly everyone there. Kizzie could hear it in the murmurs of several people at nearby tables.

Miss Bessie continued.

The loss of that land wouldn't have just been the death of Smithville and Clement but a heritage that can be traced back for a hundred years. Did the people up at the Capitol give a hoot? No, they didn't care.

But let me tell you people, God works in mysterious ways and He had a plan. Her audience agreed:

"Yes he did."

"Amen."

"Yes sir, tell 'em Sista."

"Thank you Jesus."

"That's when our Kizzie found her way home the first time. We don't know why God laid it on her heart to come back to visit at that particular time; we don't know why He chose her to be the Angel to work out the miracle we all needed and had prayed for. We don't know why He put her in the right place at the right time to intercede for us. That's her story to tell if she wants to. All we know is that He did. And today, because of her, we have our farms, our businesses, a way to keep our homes and feed our children. Far from being a dying town, we are growing and thriving. We have better lives and we can look forward to a much better future.

She motioned Kizzie to join her at the podium.

"We are here today because we want to say thank you – first to God and then to you Kizzie. As the Mayor said yesterday, our hearts are filled with gratitude. We owe you a debt we can never repay. I know I speak also as the Mayor did for everyone of us when I say we love you. We appreciate you, child. You may think what you did was a small thing but if you look out over this crowd you won't find one who doesn't think it was extraordinary. You cared about this town and the people in it. You got involved. Your willingness to step in and make a difference has impacted the life of every face you see. No words could ever, ever be enough to tell you how much that means to all of us.

So it is truly my honor, Baby, and a privilege to present to you this key to our town. We are extremely proud of the woman you've become. It is our hope that this key will forever remind you that here you have friends who will always love and cherish you. And we also hope you know how much we welcome you and trust you will always want to call Smithville home.

The thundering applause went on and on. Kizzie couldn't hold back the tears that insisted on swimming to the surface of her eyelids to spill over down her face.

She was ashamed that she had thought this event trivial, unworthy of her time and attention. So many people had obviously given much of their time to months of planning to make this a special day of recognition and honor for her.

She had dreaded it since Cocoa first called to tell her, wrapped up in her own selfish emotions. It was time to acknowledge with complete sincerity their hard work but above all to respectfully return their gestures of love and appreciation.

Kizzie swiped at her tears, glad that it was also too hot for makeup. She could imagine the kind of sight she would have made with smeared eyeliner mixed with tears dripping down her face.

Somehow though, looking out at the wonderful sea of faces, she didn't think anyone of them would have cared in the least.

She took the key offered to her by Miss Bessie. It was about two feet long and six inches high, made of a thin layer of brass.

The top line on the copper plate attached in the middle read 'To Kizzie Elizabeth Carpenter'. A line underneath read 'With love and gratitude we proudly present this Key to the town whose life you helped restore'. A third line read ' The People of Smithville, Virginia – June 30, 1978'.

She folded the heavy key to her heart as she switched places with Miss Bessie.

She didn't have a clue how to begin so she did what had always served her best. She opened her mouth and began.

"Hello everyone."

They all yelled back. "Hey there Kizzie." The anxiety was gone immediately. She was among friends.

"You all have truly outdone yourselves. I am deeply touched and humbled that you feel I am worthy of such an honor. The celebration and welcome home yesterday, now this wonderful picnic today...I don't know what to say. Except this IS my home. I was born and raised here and while I didn't come back as often as I should, it has always been home in my heart. And you all are my family. I don't know either, why I was graced with the opportunity to make a difference but it was a privilege I will always cherish. And knowing what it has meant to all of you makes it that much more important to me. Thank you from the bottom of my heart for your kind and generous welcome."

She took a deep breath.

"Now let's eat. I'm starving."

There was more applause. Kizzie reached over and hugged Miss Bessie before moving from the podium back to her seat. Cocoa was on her feet, clapping and beaming.

So were Miss Mazie, Big Jake and all the others. Looking at them her heart felt lighter than it had in years. This really was her family. No words were necessary for her to know that.

She turned to see Zak standing with Thomas on the sound stage. They both were whistling, clapping and making cat calls at her, smiles as big as an ocean.

She made faces at them but the beam on her own face told them how little she meant it. Instead of feeling embarrassed, she felt happiness, marred only by her inability to return the hug from Seal.

The day was filled with music and food. Kizzie hadn't believed it possible to have that much fried chicken in one place. There couldn't be a chicken left alive in the entire county.

And she ate with abandon; until she thought if she took another bite it would run out of her throat. She couldn't remember the last time she had enjoyed the simple act of enjoying a meal.

Thomas loaded the reel to reel with a pre mixed dance tape, then he and Zak joined Cocoa and Kizzie at the table. Zak had changed from his uniform into matching linen slacks and short sleeve shirt.

This time a thin belt, matching the sandals from the night before, split the outfit through the middle nicely.

They had finished eating. The three of them were giving Kizzie the official tour of the park, teasing her unmercifully about her 'star' status. Cocoa and Thomas took turns telling her how hard it had been for the jean company to convince the town council their offer was genuine.

When word had spread that there was a chance to stop Harriman from extending the highway, chaos didn't adequately describe the reaction. Half of them wanted to snatch at it before the offer came off the table, the other half called them all fools for letting themselves be hood winked by the devil walking around in jeans.

The company insisted their negotiations with Miss Eddie remain secret until after the deal was done. Miss Eddie didn't have a problem with that but the gossipers had a field day when Miss Eddie started 'acting funny'.

Normally, she couldn't be dragged more than a few miles from her diner. Mayor Dennis had literally choked on a donut when he walked into the council meeting and saw Miss Eddie already seated at the head of the table. He wasn't about to tell her she had to leave.

It was right after that meeting when the visiting artist arrived to paint her portrait.

None of them had known about Kizzie's role, at her request, until construction was begun on the warehouse.

The council hired an attorney to safeguard the interests of the town. What the lawyer was really there to do was to protect them all from each other's disagreements about everything from whether to use glass or stone or both in the design right down to how far down to put the cement flooring.

Before the ink was dry on the mountain of paperwork and contracts, the trucks, cranes, backhoes and all types of equipment began to show-up. One year and nine months later the newest 'citizen' of Smithville was born.

They walked and talked. Zak or Thomas would point out the locals, refreshing Kizzie's memory about the townspeople she had long ago forgotten.

Everyone wanted to shake her hand and she gladly obliged.

As they pointed out certain people Cocoa would fill in the gossip. This married couple who slept together but not with each other, or this boyfriend that got stuck in the closet when the real boyfriend showed up early, or that's old man Joe Otis-he had to sleep out here in the park for a week because he couldn't explain to Mrs. Otis why he showed up at four o'clock in the morning without his false teeth.

This was the same Joe Otis who had been complemented on how nice his teeth looked by one of the auxiliary ladies. He had helped her take groceries from the basket and loaded them on the moving register in the supermarket. Without so much as a pause, he had reached into his mouth and taken out the top row. "Here, you like 'em. You can take 'em."

"Well! I never...

"Well I never either but I thought I'd try it."

The woman ringing up the groceries laughed so hard she had to ring up several items twice.

They walked and talked and laughed some more. Kizzie didn't realize how far until she saw the building in front of her.

"Told you you hadn't seen the best yet," Zak said.

It was the new mill; a beautiful piece of architecture made of brick along the bottom which housed the reception area and the factory; glass across the upper half camouflaged the well designed offices on the second floor.

It was completely modern and no expense had been spared. Kizzie saw Jill's hands all over the blueprint of this building; from the paved stone front patio to the matching stone columns.

It actually was an extension of the park. They had followed the path from the park down a set of stone steps built into the slope of the farthest end of the park, away from the tents.

Looking up, another surprise! The tall doors, made of thick glass, anchored on each side by wide panels of glass that reached out to the brick walls, extended well above the first floor roof line.

The hours of operation were displayed in small print on one side of the door handle and the building address was on the other. Above the doors a half moon panel of glass was inset into glazed granite.

Chiseled onto the glass had been added 'The Carpenter Mill'. Built-in lights reflecting off the glass insured the name could be read day or night, even from the new highway.

But what impressed Kizzie most was the hand carved plaque permanently mounted at eye level on the left column. Kizzie read. The Carpenter Mill – Established June 30, 1977 – In Loving Memory of Dallas and Elizabeth Carpenter.

Kizzie didn't know what to say so she just stood there. She couldn't think of any other single event that had made her as happy. It was the perfect tribute and nothing the town had done could ever have meant more to her.

She didn't think her heart could take anymore. She ran her hand over the plaque several times then crossed her arms in a self hug.

Zak watched the smile cross her face and the tears roll in silence down her cheeks. His heart whispered 'we love you' at the same time that Cocoa hugged her from behind just as she had that morning. "Exactly one year ago today."

For once, Thomas was silent as he looked on.

"I told you we all pay our debts Kiz. Mr. Dallas and Miss Lizzie were beloved members of this town. We all knew they would be as proud of you as we are.

We also knew how much you loved them. To have this building dedicated to their memory would be the greatest tribute we could make to you.

Zak added, "this is the one single thing the whole town agreed on unanimously; not one dissenting vote."

With that he took Kizzie's hand to lead her back to the tents. "You'll get the full tour tomorrow. Jimmie Eggleston has repeated his script so many times I think he could describe everything in the place with his eyes closed. But he gets just as excited showing everyday people around today as he did a year ago.

I wouldn't miss what he has in store for you for all the sex in New Orleans!!"

Cocoa and Thomas were a few feet ahead. "Get a move on you two. We're holding up the party!"

The tables had been moved to the grass, clearing the wooden dance floor in each tent. The dancing, drinking, lying, laughing and otherwise good times went on until well past midnight. Zak managed to steal a couple of slow dances with Kizzie.

He must have looked like real comic relief, trying to hold her close and at the same time trying to keep the bulge in his pants at a respectable distance. After a few tries at that he gave up. He folded her in his arms the way he'd wanted to since childhood.

She seemed relaxed as they made small talk. If she noticed the wild thumping of his heart she was kind enough not to rib him about it. At least not right then. She wasn't sure if it was leftover fireworks or butterflies still going off in her stomach. Whatever it was she decided she liked the feeling.

Except for taking away the tons of leftover food, everyone was told to leave everything as it was. The clean up committee would finish the next day, after church services of course.

Reverend Newhouse wasn't pleased that Kizzie had begged off from attending the services but he assured her she was forgiven; after all it was her first Sunday back and he was sure there would be many more opportunities for her to catch one of his sermons.

Zak stayed to help Tommy B the deejay repack the stacks of albums and cassette tapes so they were the last to leave.

Kizzie took advantage of having Cocoa to herself.

"You look absolutely stunning Coe. I can't believe the weight you've lost."

Cocoa was wearing the signature hi heels. These were tan and made out of leather that looked like straw. Her jean skirt hit the middle of her thighs.

The off the shoulder pheasant blouse was a mixture of animal prints, cinched at the waist with a wide belt that matched the sandals. It was one of the rare times she lost the smooth ponytail.

Today, loose curls shone as they fell around her shoulders, framing her face perfectly. She was indeed stunning.

"Hush your mouth girl. You only saying that cause it's true." It was so easy to laugh with Coe. "But girl, talk about losing the weight…if you think it was hard trying to get the folks in this town to agree on anything, try taking off thirty pounds. But when I couldn't see 'girlfriend' down there anymore I said Oh Hell No. This shit has got to go."

And you know the first pounds I shed came right off the breastesses, as Thomas likes to call them. But girl, I didn't mind at all cause I still got nice Cleaveledge, Thomas again. The day I hit those scales and saw those thirty pounds of dead fat gone, I bent over in the bathroom, stuck my head as far between my legs as I could and said hello to 'girlfriend'...Helloooo Vagina. It's so damn good to see you, where the hell you been? I'd almost forgot what you look like."

"Hey, what's so funny over there?"

"Mind your business Thomas."

"You are my business, woman! Didn't I teach you nothing yet!"

"Girl you ought to just stop. Saying hello to your vagina!! Only you!!! They were still laughing when Zak and Thomas put the last of his equipment back in his truck.

It wasn't long after they had everything packed away that Cocoa started in on Zak.

"Hey Zak? Did you tell Kiz about the time Thomas wanted to get back at me for some man he thought he saw me with?"

Thomas had been talking trash all evening. Zak couldn't miss a chance of giving him back some of his own medicine.

Thomas threw away his cigarette and sat at the table where Kizzie had sat earlier. He pulled Cocoa down to the bench beside him. Kizzie sat across from them. Zak remained standing.

"Damn Zak, you ain't gonna tell her that story are you?"

Zak didn't even pretend to ignore him.

"See Kiz. Thomas was always talking 'bout how he had all these women who treated him like a king before Cocoa came along. He'd hang out in the clubs and just have women all over him. He'd say 'come 'ere Baby with yo' fine self. Hmmm! Hummph! Girl, that chocolate is looking good! Don't you know what that stuff does to a man?" I'm gonna get me a woman to take home tonight.

"It didn't matter if he had a steady woman or not. He loved them all. One time he got mad at Cocoa 'cause he claimed she was out with some low life piss head – that's what he called him. "Unhh Huh, go 'head. You think you the only one can get a little stuff on the side. I can get one too. He bragged to Cocoa 'bout when I get through putting it on her, I'mma let her show you how to treat a man sometimes."

Well, it just so happens that we were all going over to this new place called Three Points somewhere over near Clement".

Cocoa couldn't stand it. "Let me tell her, let me tell her," already laughing.

Thomas, knowing what was coming, was already mumbling some kind of defense…"Now see, ya'll know you ain't right to go telling Kizzie some messed up shit like that, when it was ya'll's fault I got all jammed up anyhow."

Cocoa couldn't help it. "Our fault?" We didn't tell you to go after the first woman you saw in that club. And it wasn't us who bought her a drink. That was your own doing. You were gonna get you a woman and you got one." Both she and Zak were already laughing just at the memory.

Cocoa had to take deep breaths before she could resume the story.

"Now here's where the fun starts Kiz. He's already told me before we even got out of the car to not get too close to him cause he didn't want anybody thinking I was his woman, messing up his program."

Her curls danced about her face as she laughed.

I said fine by me so Zak and I went on in and left his hindparts somewhere behind us. I went to find a table and Zak went to order a set-up. It took a while for Zak to get our drinks so I decided to go out on the dance floor. I come back to the table just about the same time Zak gets there with the drinks.

And I'll be damned if I don't see him strolling up with this woman who plops her ass down in my seat. I don't even know where the hell she came from.

I swear to God, Kiz, she had to be the weirdest woman you ever saw. She actually didn't look too bad from a distance. But we soon found out she was crazy as hell. She was almost as tall as Zak and skinny and real dark skinned, with a black one piece tight pant suit on. She had on this short cropped black wig and had gold trim around one of her top front teeth. It wasn't five minutes before she asked Thomas for a cigarette. I watched her smoke about half of it then she just reached up and put it out with her fingers. I'm hunching Zak like you wouldn't believe.

It was time to dance."

Thomas starts groaning. Cocoa ignored it.

"There weren't that many people on the dance floor so we were dancing our little asses off. All of a sudden I see this woman go down on the floor, stretched out full length like she's doing push ups with her ass stuck up in the air. In the middle of the dance floor!

I grabbed Zak by the arm and turned him around to see her. Kiz, you've never seen anything like it. I don't know what the hell this woman was doing. You should've seen the look on Thomas' face. He didn't have any idea what the hell he'd gotten himself into.

That's when he tried to run. Zak caught him before he could get away and pushed his ass back over to where she was. "Get your ass right on back over there." Everybody on the floor was laughing. They obviously knew the deal about this woman cause we found out later that the bartender had told Thomas he was going to regret buying her that drink.

Well, by now, I've got to piss so bad I can't stand it. Then this Negro has the nerve to ask me to help him. Nah!! You didn't even want me near you remember? I might mess up your program. You didn't want anybody to think I was your woman. I left him out there with her.

This other woman and me actually held each other up, laughing so hard we were doubled over trying to get to the bathroom. When we closed the bathroom door we both fell up against the wall, we were laughing so hard.

Zak took up the story. (Of course while Cocoa had been talking he was in full showmanship, recreating for Kizzie the moves the woman was making. Kizzie was laughing so hard she thought she was gonna pee on herself.)

"After they went in the bathroom, Thomas broke away and headed for the men's room. I followed him in there.

There were at least five guys, I'm not lying Kiz, all huddled in the bathroom trying to hide from this woman. Once in awhile one of 'em would stick their head out "she still out there?"

When Thomas finally thought it was safe to come out he went back to the table. She was there in a second. She sat down and stretched the upper part of her body across the table, like this, crying!!! And there's crazy ass Thomas ready to fall for that bullshit. He says 'what the hell you crying about, I mean did you just break up with your man or something'. She mumbled something but by then Cocoa was out of the bathroom and headed for the door. I was right behind her.

"Thomas, you can come if you want to Bro but we're outta here."

You could still hear people laughing when we left. But the funniest thing was Kiz, the way they all turned to look at us, as if to say, yep they're out of towners. Thomas was the first one to reach the car. When Cocoa and I got there he was sitting hunched down in the back seat with all the doors locked. I thought I was gonna have to break into my own damn car!"

They laughed together at least another ten minutes. Thomas laughing the hardest.

Not wanting to be alone with Zak, Kizzie was glad to have Cocoa there to give her a ride. Thomas already knew there would be no play for him tonight but he had to try anyway. He looked Cocoa from head to toe, licking his lips. "Hmmmm Hunnnh! You're a fine thang! He ran for the safety of his truck before Cocoa could find something to throw.

Zak said good night to Kizzie, pinching her nose. "See you tomorrow Precious." Somehow hearing the childhood name this time didn't bother her in the least.

Chapter 16

She and Cocoa were stretched out across Cocoa's bed talking about what a wonderful day it had been.

"I just want to tell you Coe. Getting back to that 'you can thank me later remark', I think there couldn't be a better time than now. You did a terrific job with everything, she said, excitement still present in her voice. "I don't know how to ever thank you. I want you to know, most of all, how grateful I am to have you as my best friend. Not just for today but our whole lives. I don't know what I would do without you."

Cocoa sat up so she could look Kizzie in the eye. "You know you don't have to thank me Kiz. Our friendship means as much to me as it does to you.

She took Kizzie by both feet and started to tickle her. "Oh no, please not the feet." Kizzie pulled her feet underneath her, Indian style.

"But I do know there's something still bothering you and I want you to know the door to Kizzie's closet, in this case, my sister arms will have to do, will be open when you're ready to talk about it." She dipped her head and peered at Kizzie from the corner of her eye.

"Hmmmn?"

Kizzie was ready. At least for this part.

"He stole from me Cocoa." She blurted. "After all I thought we had together, he stole from me!!"

"Marcus."

"Yes."

Now Cocoa knew why there hadn't been a whisper of his name since she got here. She listened.

"I knew for a long time, the last two years actually, that something wasn't right between us. Of course, I kept looking to fix me…what's wrong with me? I kept after him for months to tell me what was wrong. I knew we were no Romeo and Juliet but I thought we had something good you know? We were comfortable."

"At first, he'd just play it off like he didn't know what I was talking about. Then it got worse. He and I didn't officially live together but we had spent a lot of time back and forth at each other's place. Then he didn't want me to come over to his place anymore. He said I was just gonna nag him about cleaning up or picking up all the bills and papers laying around. He stopped coming to my place except every now and then he'd show up, trying to pretend everything was normal.

Then just after you called and invited me down here, I was going through my account, just to make sure I had everything squared away before I came down here. I don't know how I'd missed it before but there were huge sums of money missing and I couldn't remember what I'd spent it on. I asked Marcus about it and he went into a rage. That's when I accepted the truth…it wasn't me. Marcus was stealing from me. I had no idea what he was doing with the money.

So after I saw that I started checking everything. You know me…once I start a puzzle I won't stop until I've fit in the last piece. He'd taken cash out on my credit cards, written checks to himself, stole cash. That's what he was doing on the nights he would come over. He knew I didn't really go through my finances that often because with it being just me I could pretty much keep up with everything in my head.

I was so hurt Coe. But then I got mad. I went to his place. It was 2:30 in the morning.

"You rotten coward son of a bitch. You either open this god damned door or I 'll break it down with this hammer. I know you're in there."

I didn't even recognize him when he opened the door. He was usually well groomed but he looked and smelled like he hadn't had a bath in a week. The place was a wreck. He started begging as soon as I got through the door.

He actually wanted more money from me! He didn't give one good God Damn that I was there to shake the truth out of his ass.

I don't know what you did with my money and right now I don't give a rat's ass if it's gambling, drugs or the mob or whatever. But you listen to me good you load of goat shit. If you ever come anywhere near me again, I'll claw your gutless balls out with my bare hands and squeeze them in my nutcracker. You poor excuse for a human being. All the time you had me believing something was wrong with me. You make me want to puke.

I was outta there Coe. For the next month I cleaned out every piece of his ass I could find in my place and threw the shit in the garbage. It wasn't even good enough for the homeless. I shook his ass off like he never existed. I was determined not to feel like a fool but that's easier said than done.

I had moved him out of my life but what was my life going to be now. I wrestled with that the whole month before it was time for me to come down here. That's why at the last minute I packed my Jeep and headed out. There was something better than him planned for me and I knew I would have to make a giant step to find it.

So here I am."

"Now see I'm real mad at your ass Miss Kizzie. You never breathed a word. I would've liked nothing better than to saw the nigger's dick in half with the dullest saw out in that old smokehouse."

"That is exactly why I didn't tell you. The last thing I needed was to have to bury him and then try to get you off on a murder charge. But thank you for wanting to."

"Oh girl, don't even think about it. I'm just glad you left his broke, nasty ass up there."

Cocoa reached for her with those wide open sister arms. Kizzie fell right in..She didn't cry this time. She smiled. It was just so good to be home.

Chapter 17

Zak paced the hardwood for the fifth time that morning. It was only a little after five but he had been up for most of the night. He'd paced every floorboard in every room in that house, inspecting it like he'd never been there before, even though he'd lived there more than ten years.

He was an early riser so the early hour didn't bother him, except normally he would have had at least a couple hours sleep. At three thirty he had given up.

He stepped into the shower full blast on cold water. Still, it did nothing to cool the heat in his balls and his 'johnson', swollen to the point of bursting. It had a mind of its own when it came to women but usually with some effort he could maintain some decent control. When it came to Kizzie it was a different story altogether. The one 'eye' was blind and the 'brain' was about as smart as a cabbage. It had been that way since his first erection.

Facing the mirror, he braced against the sink and hung his head. His thoughts were as scattered as his earlier pacing had been.

He had made love to his first woman on his twelfth birthday. He wasn't sure if it had been a mistake, but he'd told Big James about something that happened to him this one time when he was with Kizzie.

He and Kizzie had always been inseparable. He spent more time at the Carpenters than his own house. On the nights that Mr. Dallas would make him leave he'd pretend to go home, only to double back and come in through Kizzie's window.

One night about a month before his birthday, he had arrived at her window as she was changing clothes for bed. Usually she slept in two piece pajamas. She was ten and as a treat Miss Lizzie had bought her a big girl gown. It was pink cotton, with white lace around the neck, sleeves and hem.

Zak stuck his head through the window at the precise moment she dropped her panties and stood stark naked, enjoying the soft feel of her gown. He had seen her this way at least a hundred times.

Something was different about this one. A pain started between his legs as two small mounds grew into huge knots and the small limb into a log. The pit of his stomach felt like it was on fire. He was scared to death.

"Hi Zak," Kizzie said. "Mama got me a new gown. Wanna see?" She was proud.

He wondered how the hell she could act so normal.

"What's wrong with you," she asked impatiently. "How come you looking at me like that?"

"Nothing", he mumbled. "I...I...I gotta go."

Not knowing what was happening to him he didn't know what to do. Humiliated, he left his bike where it was and ran all the way home.

It was after he'd asked Big James about it that his father decided it was time the boy learned the facts of life. To hell with the birds and the bees. He was going to give him a taste of real honey.

He had picked Zak up on his birthday. They paid a visit to Pretty Pearl's, in some town Zak had never heard of.

He had no idea how he got there but he did remember the room. It had red velvet drapes around the walls, lit by a ton of candles. The bed was covered with a matching bedspread folded back to reveal clean white sheets. There must have been a dozen pillows.

His father had disappeared as soon as 'Candy' showed up wearing nothing more than this fluffy thing barely large enough to cover her huge nipples and so short he could see tiny hairs peeking out from the feathery bottom where her thighs ended. Big James gave specific instructions to Candy.

"The boy is green as onions. When he leaves here I want you to make sure he knows the difference between boys and girls, men and women, a real virgin and old ass pussy he ought to stay away from. Give him the whole lesson. It's his birthday. Make him a man doll face."

He didn't know how long he was in that room. When Big James came back for him he had been asleep. He didn't say a word on the way home. He did remember that for the first time, he didn't hug his father when he dropped him off. Instead he shook his hand.

His father, understanding completely, returned the handshake with a firm one of his own.

It was a man's rite of passage.

It was a week before he could bring himself to face Kizzie.

Zak raised his head to look in the mirror. Thoughts still unsettled, he massaged the short growth on his face. Taking down the shaving cup he added warm water to the soap inside and worked up a thick lather with the round shaving brush.

It had happened again the minute he spotted those legs back on Burning Cross Road; again as he sat looking at her sleeping, again when he leaned against her ear at the table; again when they were dancing.

He rubbed at the swollen log, "go down you dumb son of a bitch". It didn't go down and Zak knew another cold shower was not going to help.

He shook his head; trying to chase out the cobwebs and make himself focus on his date with her tonight. He would give his life if this date could be the one to make up for the one he hadn't kept when she was eighteen. He had broken her heart that night and tonight he was going to break it again.

Zak had known that facing Kizzie was not going to be easy. But until he had actually tried to piece the words together, he hadn't realized how tough. For the second time in his life he was terrified.

He did not scare easily. As a matter of fact he was fearless. It had started as a child when he would roam the streets of Smithville at all hours. Very few dared get in his face and if they did they wouldn't be stupid enough to do it a second time. He was street, through and through.

He'd been in more fights than he could name because his fierce pride refused to let him back down from a challenge. He'd been in drunken brawls. He'd stole cars...he'd wrecked them too. Afterwards if he needed a part to fix it up he just stole whatever he needed from another one and kept on going.

By the time he was fifteen the Sheriff had labeled him the town hell raiser.

He'd spent four years in Vietnam. He had killed when his life was threatened and never had a single nightmare. Not once had he felt real fear.

Now, as he thought about the words he would have to say to the woman he loved more than life itself, he was actually shaking so bad he had to put down the razor. "you gon' slice your own fucking throat, you moron." He decided he'd better leave the rest of the shave for another time.

But it was time to come clean with her. For all their sakes. Lies he'd allowed to fester for twenty five years had caused enough suffering. Kizzie had hated Seal all these years for things he needed to step up to, including telling her the one other incident in his life when he had been terrified. And even if it meant losing the one woman he had ever really wanted, he had to make it right.

The first lie he thought about now.

Sheriff Skinner had been forty five, five feet eight with an expanding mid-section, mainly Zak suspected because he could put away more food than any human Zak had ever seen. The man could eat! His face was round with a hairline that had already receded way past the middle of his head. Looking at his red face, it was easy to see why he was chosen each year to be Santa Claus.

But he was no Santa. If Zak was the toughest young hoodlum in town, the Sheriff had been the oldest and meanest. And strong as an ox. He had hauled Zak in so many times, he no longer tried to deny whatever the Sheriff was trying to pin on him at the time. Most of the time Zak was guilty but knew the Sheriff would have to prove it. In a few cases he was actually innocent but knew it wouldn't do any good to protest it to the Sheriff.

The Sheriff would hunt him down, probably interrupting a good time, then haul him off to his office. He'd throw him in a cell. The door would be left open. He'd keep him there sometimes just long enough to lecture him to death, then other times he'd be there for hours.

For whatever reason, he liked Zak. Maybe it was because he respected Zak's fierce pride and his guts, which reminded him so much of himself.

"Listen to me boy!"

Zak would turn over on the mattress in the cell to face the wall. The Sheriff would grab him by the nape of his neck and force him to sit upright. He'd pull up a wooden straight leg chair and sit so close Zak could smell whatever he'd eaten last.

"I said listen to me now. You're heading for trouble Son. I can see it sure as I'm sitting here. I've already been down the road you getting ready to head out on. I can tell you son. You won't find anything good waiting for you at the end of it."

The Sheriff waited a minute for it to sink in.

"The first time I hauled you in here you were thirteen with a big ass chip on your shoulder...it's still there."

Zak thought about the time the Sheriff mentioned while he let the Sheriff ramble on with his lecture.

Some high school bully, being egged on by his punk friends, had Kizzie, Cocoa and Seal hemmed up in a corner at the schoolyard. They were bragging about how they were going to rip off their panties and what they were going to do to them.

Zak had gone looking for them when they didn't show up at the bus stop. He got there just as the bully grabbed Kizzie's arm. He'd dropped his books to reach down and pick up the first thing he got his hands on; a short hickory stick some child had used for baseball.

He whailed the arm of the boy who dared put his hands on Kizzie, breaking it at the wrist. When his friends tried to gang up on him, Zak swung the bat out and didn't care what he hit.

Three boys ended up in the hospital, the other two having missing teeth and bruised ribs.

Zak told them, loud enough for the Sheriff to hear, that if either of them ever touched any one of them again, he would chop their little pickle dicks up like a carrot.

The Sheriff was saying...

"I've had to drag you down here countless times since then.

But I've never officially arrested you because I think you're good stock. You didn't need all that bullshit on your record. All you needed was a break and someone to show you what a real man is made of. I've tried to at least do that for you. But you're sixteen now Zak and pretty soon you won't be considered a minor anymore. The law will have to start looking at things different and it will be out of my hands. So you'd better start acting right, boy. Whoever it is you're mad at, let it go. It won't be worth it in the long run. For your own sake boy and for those of us who love and care about you."

Zak wanted to ask him how do you stop being mad at yourself.

That last line had gotten his attention. Except for Mr. Dallas, no man had ever told him to his face that they cared about him. Not even his father, even though he knew his father loved him.

He had been fifteen then and for the next five years, except for a few reckless driving tickets and a few scraps in bars, he had stayed out of any serious trouble. Until that one night Fate stopped smiling on him and his life changed.

It was his twentieth birthday and he was picking Kizzie up for their first real date. Zak was estatic! After a long year and a half he felt like he was getting back his Kizzie. After her parents had drowned, the light that used to shine so brightly from her soul had faded.

She had given herself completely to him that night of her parents' funeral. And taken every ounce of love he had offered her. She was forever seared in his heart. He knew, even at that age, there would never be another who could take her place.

Miss Mazie and Cocoa had insisted that she come live with them. Even so, she rarely left the house and he could count on one hand the number of times he had seen her smile. No amount of coaxing or teasing by him or Cocoa could bring her out of her shell. It was as though she had died along with Mr. Dallas and Miss Lizzie.

Then a couple of days before his birthday she showed up at his house. She let herself in wearing a smile that sent his heart over the moon.

"Let's go on a real date for your birthday."

That was it. In the days that followed, every time he saw her she seemed to be more like his Kizzie. Zak couldn't help but compare it to the time Miss Nellie had told him how she had put her brother's death in a place where she didn't have to deal with it. Life goes on.

Maybe tonight he would get his Kizzie back for good and at the same time lay his own ghosts to rest.

The day of his birthday Zak woke up humming.

He hummed as he washed his car, a five year old fifty seven Chevy he had gotten from the junkyard and fixed up himself. He polished it to a sparkle.

He was humming when he stopped by Mr. Young's to pick out the prettiest rose in the store.

He was humming when he stopped in at Old Man Stoney's to ask him to set up a special table, complete with white table cloth and real silverware.

"I don't want none of that plastic shit you be giving your regular customers either, he'd told Stoney. This is for my girl."

"You gon' finally go after that honeycomb boy?"

"Now see, it's talk like that could get a man hurt. But I feel so good today, I'mma let that one slide. You just have my table ready when I get here tonight. Eight o'clock."

At the door, Marcel Hawkins – the same bully who had grabbed Kizzie in the schoolyard all those years ago – stepped in front of him.

"Yeah, he gon' get some of dat honey. Want me to tell ya how it tastes, he said, as he sucked the two fingers on his right hand

"Zak," Stoney warned.

Not soon enough. Zak had dropped the rose. He had Marcel on the floor with his knee at his chest. His left hand was on his throat and the right drawn back ready to see him take his last breath.

Stoney caught Zak's arm in the air. "He ain't worth it son." Zak remembered where he had heard those same words before. He rose, kicking Marcel in the balls for good measure then walked out the door.

Zak rarely wore a suit.

Not today. It was his birthday. He was taking Kizzie on a real date. He left nothing out. The suit was charcoal gray. The shirt was white, lightly starched and pressed right down to the button holes. His tie, the same color as the suit, made a small knot at his throat and fell perfectly straight inside the single breasted jacket. His shoes shone in strong competition with the fifty seven Chevy.

He was ready. Making sure he didn't forget anything, he took his keys from the hall table, checked for his wallet...check. He stopped at the kitchen where he thought he had put the rose.

"Oh shit, Oh shit, Oh shit!"

"Calm down Zak, he told himself. "Calm down." He broke record speed as he headed for Stoney's. Tonight he could care less if he got a ticket. He was not going to be late.

Halfway into town he saw the lights. He started not to stop then thought better about it.

"Make it quick Sheriff", he said to himself.

Sheriff Skinner walked slowly to the driver's side of the car. Zak could tell by the look in his eye that he was not in the mood for bullshit.

"Can we make this quick Sheriff? I'm really in a hurry."

"In a hurry for what Zak?"

"Well, not that it's any of your business but I've got a date tonight. Eight o'clock. Tell you what, I'll stop by tomorrow and you can give me two tickets!"

"I know about your date Zak. The way you've been walking around here for the past two days, the whole town knows by now.

They're probably all crowded into Stoney's right now to see what you look like when you show up."

The Sheriff was silent.

"Well, come on Sheriff. Gotta go!!!"

"I'm awfully sorry Zak but I've got to ask you to step out of the vehicle."

"You're kidding me right. For a speeding ticket?"

"I'm afraid it's more than that this time Zak. Marcel Hawkins was found dead a couple hours ago. His skull was cracked. He bled to death in the alley behind Stoney's. His buddies claim they saw you do it."

"And you believe those assholes?" Zak couldn't believe this was happening.

"You know it's not what I believe Zak but what I can prove. I've gotta do my job and take you in until we get this mess all worked out."

Zak was not a begging man. About the only thing bigger than his love for Kizzie was his pride.

"Please Sheriff not tonight." He pleaded now. "Please don't do this tonight."

Five hours later, precisely at a quarter to midnight, the Sheriff dropped Zak at the bus depot, a block away from Jessie White's filling station. "Good luck son." Five minutes later Seal came from around the corner and handed him a small suitcase.

The Sheriff had taken him in and for the first time the cell had been locked behind him. The sound was the last nail in the bitch of a night that was turning into his coffin. It had only taken the Sheriff three hours to piece together what most likely had happened.

He believed Zak. Marcel had probably pissed off one of his own cronies and one of them had pummeled him into the concrete. But with both of them ready to swear on a stack of Bibles that it was Zak, there wasn't much he could do. Except try to protect this bullheaded SOB from his own fool hardiness.

He had called in a favor from a friend over at Fort Grange Army base in Clement. He'd spent the next hour trying to convince Zak that he had no options. Zak finally agreed on the condition that he would never tell Kizzie. He'd insisted on the same thing from Seal when he asked her to pack his bag and meet him at the depot.

Seal begged again for the hundredth time, trying to change Zak's mind.

"You can't do this to her Zak. She'll die all over again. You've got to let me tell her. "She knew it was a waste of time.

"No."

She hugged him hard. When she let go he handed her the rose the Sheriff had picked up from Stoney's.

Without another word he took the suitcase from Seal and walked into the depot. He was still wearing his suit.

Unbeknownest to either of them, Kizzie had been running all over town looking for him. She arrived at Jessie White's just in time to see the hug with Seal and watch as he handed her the single rose.

He'd spent ten years in Uncle Sam's army. The initial six year stint which introduced him to the violence and death of Vietnam, then re-upped for another four because he had no idea what to do with his life. He made only one visit home...to bury his mother who died at the age of forty five from alcohol poisoning.

Chapter 18

Zak left the bathroom, taking the one and a half flight or stairs back down to the living room.

He stopped in the center of the room. He loved this house. It had been the Carpenters old place. He couldn't believe it when he'd come home ten years before and the house was still here, empty.

Kizzie had inherited the house when her folks died but before leaving town, she had instructed Cocoa's parents to sell it to the first person who made an offer. She didn't care about the price and didn't want the money. "Keep it if you want or give it to charity. I don't really care."

No buyers had come along. The Solomons, Seal's brothers and others in town had taken turns keeping the grass cut and maintaining the upkeep; Miss Mazie and Cocoa had tended Miss Lizzie's flowers.

Zak had bought the house. The front porch, the living room and the kitchen he'd left unchanged, except for new coats of paint and resanding and polishing the beautiful wood floors. He also had not touched a thing in Kizzie's old room. From time to time he would spend the night in there, on his usual place on the floor, just to feel close to her. He never slept in the bed.

He *had* changed Mr. Dallas and Miss Lizzie's room. It was at the end of the hallway from the top of the stairs, opposite Kizzie's. The bathroom was in between.

He and Thomas had knocked out the walls of the bathroom and the small bedroom, enlarging them both. A wall of windows ran the entire length of the back of the house. Those for Kizzie, he hoped. She loved windows!

A set of French doors opened to the upstairs porch he'd added onto the bedroom. He'd also spent more than a few nights out there, praying for the day he would see her again.

Well, now the day was here and ironically he wished he had more time.

Noticing the time on the kitchen wall clock was six thirty, he used the wall phone to call Joe, his Deputy.

When he had left Kizzie at the picnic, he'd gone in to check on two local trouble makers he'd locked up Friday night right after the celebration.

They'd gotten drunk and crossed the line from celebrating to disturbing the peace when they started to beat up on each other over at Stoney's. This wasn't their first time and in spite of theirselves, Zak was trying to do for them what Sheriff Skinner had for him.

He'd also told Joe that he would not be in uniform for the next couple days and he expected Joe to keep the roof on the town.

Deputy Joe was quite capable of handling things on his own but Zak called him anyway. He wanted to tell him it was ok to release the two boys. He was also hoping something had come up that Joe would need him for.

He knew already that he was going to have too much time on his hands today.

Joe assured him he had everything under control.

Knowing Joe, hearing that news made Zak feel both relief and worry.

Zak hung up the phone. He went back upstairs to finish his shave. He managed to get the job done this time without slicing his own throat.

He moved down the hall to the bedroom and slipped on an old tee shirt with some raggedy jeans.

Back downstairs he went through the house again. It was as spotless as the last time he checked it.

Finding nothing that needed to be done inside, he bounced out the back door. On his way he stopped to grab a pair of cutting shears from the hook inside the pantry door.

Outside, he made the same assessment. He'd already cut the grass and watered the flowers. Miss Mazie would use those scissors on him if even one pedal on those flowers died for lack of watering.

Around the corner he spotted the car. The same fifty seven Chevy he had planned to pick Kizzie up in all those years ago. It too was spotless. Parked next to it was his pick-up.

He crossed the driveway. Using the shears he cuts three handfuls of pink and white peonies then headed for his truck. He tossed the flowers on the seat beside him.

Without license or wallet he started the pickup and backed out of the driveway.

With one chore in mind but no other particular destination planned Zak drove.

A few people were already milling about in town, even at this early hour as he drove down Main street. Turning at the corner between Jessie White's and the bus depot, he took the service road past Hillside Park and the new mill.

He parked at the front entrance to the cemetery. He'd been out here any number of times so he knew exactly where to find the grave sites. He took the flowers from the seat, then the ax and a pair of gloves from the bed of the truck. He worked first on his mother's grave, digging weeds and pulling wild grass.

His father, now almost seventy, had remarried a long time ago. He lived near Rawlins but no longer drove. Zak would visit him from time to time but Big James had never asked Zak to bring him out to visit his first wife's grave.

He laid one of the bouquets at his mother's headstone.

He walked over several sites until he found the headstones for Mr. Dallas and Miss Lizzie, side by side in eternity as they had been in life. He cleared away the weeds. He threw out the old flowers then placed a fresh bouquet in each of the cups he had permanently buried near each of their headstones.

On other visits, Zak would talk to Miss Lizzie about any number of things on his mind but mostly about Kizzie. "I let you both down Miss Lizzie. I didn't look out for her like I promised. Now I don't know if I'll ever be able to make it up to her."

He knew they couldn't hear him but somehow it always made him feel better just to verbalize the words to them.

Leaving the grave sites, he walked toward the back of the graveyard that ended several yards before the hill gave way to a slope heading down to the river. Three small fishing boats and one canoe were anchored to the pier but no one was in sight.

Zak walked to the end of the pier. He sat down on the bench, his legs outstretched and his hands folded behind his head.

The day was warm, the air moist, but still the sky was overcast. The sun had not yet broken its way through the clouds.

Zak didn't know how long he sat there, undisturbed. He imagined most folks were still in church. But he was still surprised that no one had shown up to cast their lines.

Finally able to focus his thoughts he had rehearsed over and over what he planned to say to Kizzie. No matter how he worded it, he was certain of one thing; there was no changing the outcome.

He stood and walked to the edge of the pier, watching the currents bob and weave as the wind moved across the water.

He wouldn't exactly call himself a religious man but in his heart he acknowledged that he was going to need help.

He didn't know much about the protocol for prayer but he had been around the people of Smithville enough to know that they believed in miracles.

He was desperate enough now that if praying could make a difference he was ready to give it a shot. He fell to his knees, right there on the pier.

His prayer was simple.

"Heavenly Father, I don't know if I've earned the right to ask you for help. I've done some things that I know probably pissed you off real good. But I'm not asking for me today Lord. It's for my Kizzie. She's tying to get her old self back Lord, but she's still hiding so much of her pain. She doesn't even know it. And when I tell her the truth tonight I'm not sure I will ever get her back. But I'm asking you God, help her to let go her pain. If you can't see your way clear to let her love me again, please God, please please, at least let her forgive me. Not for my sake God but for her. Forgiveness is for her so that she can be happy again, smile like she used to. That smile I would die for. I will gladly accept whatever you dish out to me Lord, but please just let her have peace."

He didn't know what else to say.

Zak rose slowly. He turned and walked back toward the truck. There was nothing else he could do.

Chapter 19

Cocoa insisted on helping Kizzie get dressed for her date with Zak. Right now she was trying to add curls to her hair.

Kizzie wasn't wild about the idea. "Last time I looked, I was the oldest. And the time before that I looked I could still dress myself."

Cocoa fired right back. "Dressing yourself – score two points. I have about thirty five kindergartners who do it every day. But dress yourself like a knockout, that's Cocoa's department."

"Why on earth would I care about being a knockout? It's Zak. The same Zak you turned me into a knockout for the last time, who never showed up. And by the way who I didn't see again until two days ago. Do you remember that Miss Cocoa? It only happened to be a measly twenty five years ago."

Cocoa's normal patience was wearing very thin.

"Turn around. You're farting around so much, you're gonna make me burn you with these curlers."

Kizzie sat still. She looked at herself in the mirror on Cocoa's vanity table.

"Whatever it is he's so all fired up to tell me Coe, is just going to be a bunch of excuses for why he didn't look for me all those years. I don't need the lies. It took me more than two years to admit that Marcus was just using me. I finally found the courage to do what I needed to do for me to walk away from him. Zak's already had his turn at doing the same thing to me. Why should I open up the way for him to do it to me again?"

Her voice was strained.

Giving up on the idea of curls Cocoa put the curlers in the holder on the table. She leaned forward against the back of the chair so that she could face Kizzie's image in the mirror.

"Now you listen to me Miss Kizzie Carpenter." Cocoa's tone sounded very much like Miss Lizzie.

"Don't you dare try to lay the whole thing in Zak's lap. Yeah, it took him a while to come back here to face up to you and the rest of us. That wasn't easy for him. I don't know which of you two have the most stupid pride. But you hear this Miss Kizzie. The first person he asked about was you. And he hasn't stopped asking. It was you as I recall who threatened to 'yank out my pretty white ponytail' if I even hinted to him where you were or how to reach you. Do you remember that Miss Kizzie?"

Not having any response that made sense Kizzie lowered her eyes from the intensity in the mirror.

Cocoa thought she might as well go ahead and say what she thought Kizzie had needed to hear for years.

"Besides Kiz, the man loves you desperately. He worships you. I've never seen or heard about any man who loves a woman with such, such...abandon. And he has no shame about it! He screams it to anybody who will listen! He's done it from the time you were six years old. Sure, he hurt you when he left, but maybe he had a reason and maybe it wasn't his choice. Maybe you need to let go of your own self pity long enough to consider that you're not the only one who's been hurt here. You've been so careful to wrap up your pain and tuck it carefully away, thinking that's the answer, that you're blind to the idea that the rest of us might have just as much pain that we can't tuck away.

What you fail to see, my sister, is that it's only masked over. Until you deal with it, it will never leave you. You'll carry it around like a stone around your neck until it turns you into stone. What you also fail to see is that there is only one way to deal with..."

She swirled the chair around from the mirror and stooped to look up at Kizzie. She saw the tears simmering but she didn't back off. She loved her like her own sister.

"Just one way, Kiz."

Kizzie looked at her, her mouth trembling.

"Let love have its way Kizzie. It's way past time."

After several minutes Kizzie breathed deeply. She leaned forward and kissed her friend's forehead.

"You'd better finish making me gorgeous before I blame you for making me late."

"That's my girl. Turn around."

Chapter 20

Zak was right on time according to Kizzie's timeclock. At quarter of eight Cocoa announced up the stairs "Romeo's here."

Of course by now Thomas had arrived. He was leaning against the stairwell next to Cocoa. Miss Mazie and Miss Suzie had dropped by 'just to check on everybody'. Nobody was fooled.

She came down the stairs just as Zak came into the front hall.

"Great" he thought. An audience is the last thing he needed. He immediately forgot about all of them when he spotted Kizzie.

She was a heavenly vision. Her dress was black silk and the fit was perfect. The wide fabric across each shoulder met in soft folds across the top of her breasts. The bra bodice connected a tent shaped skirt, with small pinch pleats underneath her breasts that caused the skirt to cascade to just above her knees.

The shoes were strapless black sandals with rhinestone straps between the toes.

Her hair was done up in a beautiful French roll with tiny strands peeking out at her neck and framing her face.

The rhinestone earrings were long and thin almost reaching her shoulders. She wore no necklace.

Her smile, matching his, was outshining the rhinestones.

No pretense, it took Zak a minute to catch his breath.

"WOW! WOW! Be still my heart! I'd better go back and clean myself up for this beautiful woman! Oh my God!"

He was glad he had worn his new suit. It was black with wide subtle pin stripes and off white shirt. He wore no tie but he was no slouch either.

Thomas couldn't help himself. "OK Zak you can stand there like a fool if you want to but I'mma have to help this incredible woman down the stairs."

As Thomas started forward, Zak moved. "Touch my girl tonight and you die where you stand." He never even looked at Thomas. He couldn't take his eyes off Kizzie long enough.

"Hey man, you know I was talking 'bout this woman right here by my side", Thomas said as he grabbed Cocoa's hand with a bow, kissing it twice.

"Thomas, you're hopeless." Kizzie said as she maneuvered the last two steps, accepting Zak's outreached hand. Cocoa seconded it.

"That's the God's truth."

All any of them could do was laugh.

The two sisters hovering in the living room pretended they were occupied. Kizzie knew they had missed nothing.

The four of them were right on Zak and Kizzie's heels as he walked her out to the door of the Chevy, already open and waiting for her. It was hard to tell who was grinning more, them or Zak.

The ride to Stoney's was uneventful, except Kizzie did have to remind Zak at least half a dozen times that he really should keep his eyes on the road if he wanted to get them both there alive. She may as well have saved her breath.

It was the same story at Stoney's. The parking lot was jammed with cars. One spot had been left open at the front of the building...a sign was posted –Reserved for Zak and Kizzie. Inside Zak had to maneuver himself and Kizzie through the crowd. Everyone was laughing and clapping. The men slapped Zak on the back as he passed.

"I'm gonna kill Stoney." Zak said.

"Oh no. He's already going to be dead by the time you get to him." Kizzie answered.

Just then Stoney showed up with Joe in tow. "Right this way Miss Kizzie. We've got a special table for ya'll."

"Stoney, where the hell did all these people..."

He didn't have to finish. Stoney pointed his finger directly into Joe's chest.

"Your walking newspaper over here broadcasted to everybody he saw today that you had worn Miss Kizzie down and she was going out with you tonight."

"And just why is that so newsworthy?" Kizzie wanted to know.

Joe chimed in. "Well, everybody in town knows the Sheriff's been waiting for you to turn up. Why half of 'em were here twenty five years ago...Zak cut him off with his eyes. Joe got the message.

"Anyway, he's been like a hog in slop ever since he got word you were coming. Don't you know...

It was Stoney that cut him off this time. "What I know is these two young people didn't come out here to listen to your flap half the night." He moved Joe to the side and led Zak and Kizzie to their table.

Kizzie was impressed. Still, she hadn't missed what Joe had started to say. She decided she would wait to see if Zak volunteered to tell her what he was talking about.

Stoney had cordoned off the back section of the restaurant with red velvet rope. There was one table, set for two, in the corner. The tablecloth was white and a black overlay covered the top. A single large candle burned in the center. One single red rose stood in a crystal vase on her side of the table. It had been exactly as Zak had ordered it twenty five years before.

Chapter 21

Kizzie knew where she was long before the house was visible.

The porch light was on, casting a soft glow on the swing at one end and the patio furniture on the other.

"Our old house. You're the one who bought our old house." She looked over at Zak as he shifted the gear to park.

"I did." Zak swelled with pride. "I've always loved this house. I have nothing but loving memories of everything about it."

He opened the door for her. "When I came back and saw that it was still for sale, I bought it without a second thought. "Come on. I want you to see it." He took the boxed desert from the restaurant and carried it with them inside.

Except for feeling like being on display in a fishbowl, their dinner had been wonderful. Solomon and Burke had prepared it and brought it over themselves, telling Stoney that their celebrity couldn't be seen eating anything that came out his grease spot. Stoney reminded Solomon that the two of them had eaten there often enough and look how they turned out.

Burke served delicious grilled catfish, chive seasoned creamy mashed potatoes, fried green tomatoes and warm, fluffy rolls. Neither Zak nor Kizzie could finish the meal. They waved off desert, warm lemon pudding cake, which Solomon boxed and insisted they take with them for later.

They had talked for more than two hours. He told her some of the ridiculous stuff he ran into as Sheriff and she told him about some of the wonderful people she met on her travels, like the Lakota Indians.

Zak held the front door open. She climbed the steps as though in slow motion. She didn't have to go any further than the front hallway before the crush of memories hit her like a fist to her gut.

She hadn't been here since the day Miss Mazie had Zak and the twins move all of her things over to the Sullivans.

Zak was right there beside her.

"If being here is too much for you Kizzie, we can go someplace else."

"No. No. I'm fine. I'm glad I'm here." He didn't look convinced. She tried harder. "Really, I'm ok. It's just that there was so much love in this house. So many memories. So much fun! I can't remember a time I've been happier. And how much I've missed it."

"Remember the first time you met Cocoa? We were playing jacks right there on the front porch. She slugged you because you asked her about her hair."

Zak rubbed his jaw. "I'll never forget. It reminds me to always stay on her good side."

Kizzie was feeling a little more at ease.

Zak showed her the house, ending the tour at her old bedroom.

"It's just the same," she said to no one in particular. "How can I ever thank you Zak. I would never have been able to come back here on my own."

"You don't have to thank me. It's yours. It's always been. I don't think I could have handled seeing anyone else living here. If someone else had bought it when I came back I would have paid whatever price they wanted to get it back."

He left her on her own to explore her old room.

He brought a tray of glasses and mixed drinks from the kitchen. He sat it on the patio coffee table then lowered himself down into the rocker.

She emerged through the French doors. "Oh, it's wonderful Zak. I love the addition. You and Thomas did a great job."

He handed her a glass and raised his own. "To Mr. Dallas and Miss Lizzie."

She raised her own. "I'll drink to that."

He waited until she had lowered her drink. "I need to talk to you Kiz."

"Yeah, so you've said." She sat down on the loveseat across from his rocker.

He rubbed his hands in front of him and paced several minutes before he could push the first words from his gut.

He pulled the rocker around so he sat facing her. He took both her hands in his. For a few minutes he stared at their hands, joined, as he rubbed her knuckles with his thumbs.

He raised his head slowly to look in her eyes.

"Kizzie, I love you more than life itself. I can't remember a time when I haven't loved you. I open my eyes in the morning and I see your face. I think about you a million times every moment I'm awake. My dreams are about you every night. Mr.Dallas and Miss Lizzie knew that. They trusted their most precious treasure to my care. I promised them like I'm promising you. I will always, always love you Kizzie Carpenter."

She was silent, her heart racing.

Zak went on.

"It's because I love you.....he couldn't do this.... I need you to know the truth about some things, Precious. Things that I've tried to hide from and run from for years. First, I want you to know that I would rather die than to do anything to deliberately hurt you."

He stood up, facing the screen on the porch.

"I know you've been hurt Kiz. Way more than any one person should have to endure. I know I've been to blame for some of that hurt. But I also know about some of your other hurt. I know about your brother."

He saw her wince. "Who told you?"

"Miss Nellie did. A long time ago. I can tell you later what she told me. I kept hoping you would talk to me about him. When you didn't I guessed it was still too painful for you. I decided I would wait til you were ready.

But then everything else happened; your parents, my leaving, your leaving and that time never came."

He came back to take her hands again.

"I also know what your 'Uncle' Henry did to you."

Kizzie put her hands up to cover her face. Zak pulled them down.

"That's not your shame Kizzie. It's his. I only know because that night..." he hesitated. "That night, after we made love, I know there should have been more blood."

She was humiliated again.

"Kizzie."

"Kizzie."

She looked at him.

"If the bastard wasn't already dead, I'd kill him myself."

Uncle Henry, Miss Lizzie's no good ass half brother, had molested Kizzie when she was seven. The creep had seen how much Kizzie loved for her brother to ride her on his back. Four years later he had asked her if she wanted a ride. She was so excited. For the first two or three times, nothing happened.

Then one evening as it was getting dark, he was riding her. She felt his hands inside her panties. She had tried to move away but he wouldn't let her down. He'd used his middle finger to probe inside her panties. He'd pushed so hard he had broken her virginal covering.

She was so ashamed and in so much pain the she went straight to the closet where she cried herself to sleep. He'd told her that if she ever told anyone, he would hurt her again. She didn't tell then and did everything she could to stay out of his way. It was years later that Cocoa had coaxed it out of her.

Zak had coaxed it out of Cocoa.

Zak had come home soon after Cocoa's visit five years before. All the buzz in town was about how Kizzie had cussed out Henry Perkins right in church. The story was that Kizzie was leaving church when she came face to face with Henry.

The sleeve to his right arm was folded back from his elbow to shoulder and a black cylinder with two claw hooks on the end was attached. His arm had been severed by a logging machine when his jacket got caught in it and no one was around to turn it off.

Henry had the audacity to tell her to come give him big hug. Kizzie had stared at him for the longest, disgust written all over her face.

"Don't come near me and don't you dare touch me, you scummy son of a bitch. I'm glad that arm got chewed off. If it was up to me, the machine would have been turned up to full speed and chewed up the rest of your rotten ass. It still wouldn't have been half of what you deserved."

With that, she had hauled off and laid one up side his head the entire church could hear. She then turned on her heels and left. She left town the same day.

Kizzie still felt ashamed. "I didn't want you to ever know about that. I had such hate for that man and so much shame for me. I couldn't help but wonder what other girls he had preyed on."

"Kizzie, Precious. There were never supposed to be any secrets, remember? And you didn't do a thing wrong. I wish you had told me so I could have chopped off the bastard's other arm. And some other parts besides. The kid I was back then, I would have thoroughly enjoyed every minute of his suffering."

"But how did you know...about anything? I mean, before you talked to Cocoa."

"The night we made love I asked you to trust me, remember? I knew what to do to make sure you didn't get pregnant."

He smiled at the look she gave him. "Never mind how I knew."

When I got you up to go to the bathroom, and to clean you up there wasn't as much blood as there should have been...you know what I mean! I knew you hadn't been with anyone else so it stuck in my mind how that could be. I didn't' say anything then because it was such a beautiful night I didn't want to spoil it. I just wanted you to feel safe and loved, even though your parents were gone."

"When I got back years later and heard all the talk, I hemmed Cocoa and made her tell me. Don't be mad at her Kiz."

"I'm not. I'm actually glad you know."

Zak hugged her. She was so beautiful. Not just physically but her soul was beautiful. He didn't want to let her go.

But he couldn't stop. If he did he would never have the guts again to tell her.

He sat beside her on the loveseat.

"Then Mr. Dallas and Miss Lizzie drowned." He felt her shiver.

"The reason I brought all of this up Kiz is because I need you to believe me when I tell you I know about the pain in your life. I know how you've tried to bury the memories trying to bury the pain...just to feel like you at least might get a shot at happiness."

"That was part of the reason I left that night. I thought if I had stayed I would have been one more person to hurt you. Now I know I was just being a coward."

"What are you talking about Zak? You're scaring me!"

"Oh God, help me." Zak prayed for the second time in his life.

"There was never anything between Seal and me, Kizzie. The night you saw us I had called her. I asked her to bring the clothes down to the depot. She did everything she could to convince me to talk to you."

He told her the story.

"And at Stoney's tonight? That's what Joe meant about half the people there tonight were there twenty five years ago."

"The way it was set up tonight was exactly as it was supposed to be for our first date. I even had a new suit and the same car. The rose you saw me hand to

Seal was the one I'd gotten for you." He smiled but it was sad.

"Zak, why didn't you call me? I was waiting for you. I would've come. I would've helped you. I told you. I ran all over town trying to find you. When I saw you with Seal, I didn't even try to stop the bus. But I would've come! I would've gone with you."

"And that's exactly why I didn't. I didn't want your life ruined like mine was going to be. You had been meant for better things in this world Kiz. Maybe I was just holding onto a pipe dream thinking it was me.

But there was another reason. In my heart I was looking for a reason to get away. I think that's why it only took Sheriff Skinner an hour to convince me I had to go. If I had stayed I would've been forced to tell you the truth a long time ago and I was just too afraid."

"What are you trying to say Zak? Tell me, please!

He swallowed hard. His voice was so low she could barely hear him.

"All these years Kizzie I've let you believe it was Seal who was responsible for what happened to your parents. It wasn't Seal. It was me!

She pushed away from him.

"That's a lie. You're making that up. Why are you trying to cover for her?"

"I'm not making it up Kizzie. It's the truth. Please, sit down. Please. You need to hear all of it."

Zak had loved Mr. Dallas and Miss Lizzie more than his own mother and father. He thought of them as his parents just as much as Kizzie thought of them as hers. He had probably fallen in love with Miss Lizzie as soon as he'd fallen in love with Kizzie. She was so much like her. There was nothing he wouldn't have done for either one of them.

Mr. Dallas had loved to take his wife fishing. She hated it because she was afraid of the water. But she went because it pleased Mr. Dallas.

It wasn't unusual for Mr. Dallas to take any one of the neighborhood boys along on a Saturday morning, especially Zak. Other times he would just want Miss Lizzie.

On the day they drowned, Zak had arrived early to help Mr. Dallas take all the gear down to the dock. He couldn't count the number of times he'd done the same thing.

Mr. Dallas had helped Miss Lizzie into the boat. They were both teasing him as they usually did about Kizzie. "Now Zak, when you marry that girl of ours, you gonna have to make sure you take good care of her."

"You know I will Mr. Dallas."

Zak was supposed to go with them that day but he had forgotten his tackle box. Mr. Dallas had told him to 'run along and get it son. We'll wait. Them fish ain't going no place. Everything in the river is gonna be biting today. You don't wanna miss it. I promised Kizzie a mess of catfish for supper. Oh, when you come back Son, be sure to tie up that second anchor for me." Zak had promised he would.

They both smiled at him and waved as he ran back toward town. He was happy.

It had taken him longer than usual to get back. He had helped carry Miss Lizzie's gear down so he didn't have his bike

The storm came out of nowhere. One minute there wasn't a cloud in the sky, the next it was dark as midnight. Just as Zak reached the edge of town the rain started to come down in buckets. The thunder was deafening and the lightning lit up the sky.

At that moment Zak remembered the anchor. He ran for all he was worth. His face and arms were scratched and bloody from branches he couldn't see because of the rain but he didn't care. His lungs were stinging but he kept running.

He had gotten close enough to see the boat being rocked back and forth by the strong currents. Mr. Dallas was trying to steady it and hold on to Miss Lizzie at the same time.

The first anchor gave way just as the boat capsized. He was so scared he thought his heart would burst from his chest. He froze. They surfaced once and Zak could tell that Mr. Dallas was trying to calm his wife but she was so scared she was fighting against him.

Zak fell to his knees in the mud, his face streaked with tears. When he looked up they were gone.

The rain stopped just as suddenly as it had started.

He didn't know how long he stayed out there.

Seal had seen Zak running back toward the river. She knew something was wrong by the way he ran. She took off after him. When she got to the river they were already gone and Zak was still on his knees. She somehow made him repeat himself until she had an idea of what had happened. She left him there and ran back to town. Miss Mazie's house was first. She burst through the door.

Kizzie had been with Cocoa doing the Saturday morning chores. She heard Seal's mumbled explanation 'didn't tie the anchor, the boat turned over..there was nothing I could do, nothing I could do". She had assumed Seal was talking about herself helping Mr. Dallas and Miss Lizzie. She had been telling them the broken pieces she had managed to get out of Zak about her parents. She was also trying to tell them she couldn't help Zak.

In the nightmare of the days that followed, Kizzie never asked Seal to explain or Zak what happened to his face and arms.

"I swear to God Kizzie, it all happened so fast." She could hear the tremor in his voice. The scene was as vivid to him now as it had been that day.

"I froze Kizzie. I was so scared. I froze."

He fell to his knees again just as he had that day in the rain and mud. The sob started deep in his throat. He sat huddled on the floor of the porch in front of her, the pain fresh, stabbing at his heart like daggers. His head buried between his knees, he sobbed uncontrollably.

Kizzie's tears were silent. The nightmare was back to visit her again. This time it had a face.

The man she had loved and adored from her earliest memory had let her PopPop and Mama die.

She couldn't go to him. She had to get away. She walked the four houses down to the Sullivan's, her rhinestone shoes in her hands.

Chapter 22

"You listen to me Miss Kizzie Carpenter. I've loved you since the day I sat with your mother when she brought you screaming into this world. Just like she was with me when my Cocoa was born. She loved my Cocoa like she was her own too. I'm gonna talk to you now like I would want her to talk to my Cocoa if things were different."

It had been four days. Cocoa was crazy with worry. She didn't know what to do. Kizzie refused to eat. She wouldn't come out of her room without a fight. When she did come out she'd just sit in her mother's old rocker without saying a word to anyone. She had taken one phone call from her boss Jill then immediately went back to her room. When Cocoa couldn't piss her off with some smart ass comment, she was really worried. She did the only thing she knew that might help. She turned again to Miss Mazie.

Miss Mazie had gone to find Kizzie where she was sitting in the rocker.

"Your mother loved you Child. The greatest thing she wanted for you was your happiness. Because she had found happiness in her own life Child, with the man she loved. And she wanted that for you. She wouldn't want you moping around this house, forgetting how to laugh, how to live! Your mother would never hold a grudge against anyone."

Kizzie wouldn't look at her so she went on.

"There's nothing to say there was anything that boy could've done to change the outcome that day Kizzie. You understand me? Not one thing could he have done. Your folks would be the last two people in the world to blame him for what happened."

She took Kizzie's hands and lifted her from the rocker.

"Come here Child." She wrapped Kizzie in a hug that only a mother and daughter could understand.

"I know it seems like it's easier to bear if you can blame it on somebody Baby. Then you can make some sense outta things, have a reason why it happened. But we'll never know why Child. That's why you gots to let it go Baby. You lost them but so did Zak. Listen to me Baby. He also watched them go. Can you let go of your own self pity long enough to imagine what it must have been like for that boy to sat there, helpless, watching the people he loved like his own parents, drown in that river? Believing it was his fault. Then have to live with that every day for the rest of his life. Plus to know that you were going to hate him if he told you the truth. That boy lost all around. But all you can see is how much poor Kizzie is hurting. You've harbored that hurt and used it all these years as a shield to hide from the world. Let it go Baby!"

Kizzie couldn't bear it. All the ugliness she had tried to hide behind all these years, blaming it and everyone else for why she couldn't be happy, had been brought out for the whole world to see. She couldn't hide anymore. She remembered Cocoa's words to her last Sunday...Let love have its way, Kizzie. She collapsed weeping into Miss Mazie's arms.

Miss Mazie let her cry.

Then she let her know she was fed up with her self pity and her foolishness. She insisted Kizzie stand up on her own two feet, go take a shower, put on some decent clothes then come down to eat. "In that order."

"And you know what you gotta do after that."

"Yes maam." Kizzie felt better than she had in years.

Chapter 23

First she had to find Seal. It was Thursday so Seal would be at work at the Mill. She was the front desk receptionist and from everything Cocoa said she was perfect for the job.

Kizzie's heart swelled when she saw the Carpenter Mill again and remembered what the town had done for her and her parents.

Before she could get out of the car Seal had the door open. The arms open and waiting for her were wider than the door.

Now she needed to find Zak. Cocoa had told her that when she couldn't get Zak to answer the phone at his house, she had sent Thomas down to the Sheriff's office to talk to Joe.

Joe told him that Zak called in once a day to check on things but other than that he hadn't heard from him and he hadn't been back in to work.

She looked all over town. No one had seen him but word had spread and the whole town knew she was looking. "Want us to help you find him Kizzie", the twins asked when she stopped in at the Fish Swamp. "No thanks, guys. I'll just keep looking. I need to do this myself."

"Here you go again, Kizzie Elizabeth Carpenter, damn it! Didn't you just do this shit...here you go, running all over town looking for his black ass. A-GIN! She didn't ask forgiveness.

He wasn't at the park or in the old schoolyard. He wasn't working at Miss Eddie's or at Stoney's.

Miss Gertie told her..."Lord child that man has been all over this town for the past four days, doing everything we needed done. He's gon' work his poor self to death. You go on out and find him and make him take care of hisself for a change."

At the cemetery she saw the peonies, still fresh, that Zak had put there earlier in the week. Kneeling between her parents, she dumped the whole rotten mess right on Mama and PopPop. "I was the smart one you said. I could take care of myself you said. Do the right thing you said. Well...I sure wish you had drawn me a better roadmap."

Kizzie held the delightful smelling peonies under her nose. Hmmmnnn, remember how you used to love these Mama? He cut them from YOUR garden, you know. Yep. Zak."

She rearranged both bouquets and placed them back in the metal cup Zak had made. He wanted Mr. Dallas and Miss Lizzie to always have fresh flowers.

"Everyone knew Mama. Everyone except me. No one told me. All this time. But in spite of everything, Ma, he's kept the promise he made to you and PopPop. He's done his best to take care of me. Even when I was away.

Did you see what a wonderful job he did to our house? He did that for me. He knew that one day I would wake up and want to come home. He made sure it would be here for me."

(I must beg your indulgence here to stop the story for a minute to add this)

Right about now, Mr. Dallas and Miss Lizzie must be thinking 'you can't get away from them; not even in your graves...KIDS!')

Kizzie talked to both of them until she couldn't think of anything else to say.

"I'm such an idiot Mama. I am not smart at all. But I think I'm ok now Mama. Thank you for watching over Zak. We'll be alright now. Stop worrying about us."

Before she left she added one last thing... "I'll always love you and miss you both."

She followed the slope down to the pier. He was sitting on the bench, his legs spread, his hands folded behind his head.

"Hey"
"Hey."
"Hey you."
"Hey back."

She walked to him until she was standing between his feet.

"Is that spot taken?"

"Come closer and I might tell you."

Kizzie walked until her outer thighs touched the inside of his.

"I'm holding it for my girl. She won't mind long as you don't stay too long. And you can't kiss me or anything."

Kizzie bit. "You and I will have to talk about this girl later." She poked his chest. He acted hurt. For several minutes she stood there. She watched the smile grow on his beautiful face! There was love on that face. He was nodding his head slowly to her silent question.

He looked away as he slid over to make room for her on the bench.

Neither one of them said a word for a long time. They watched the water.

Zak was the first to speak.

"It took me years to find the courage to come back here." He found his voice but had to give it another minute before he could go on. "It was just down around that bend there where it happened."

She rubbed his arm. "I know Zak."

"When I got out of the Army, I got a little place over in Clement. That was as close as I could get. Every time I thought about Smithville I would actually get the shakes. Sheriff Skinner found me over there. I don't know why that man was so good to me. I certainly didn't deserve it. About a year or so after I left he got word to me that Marcel Hawkins' cronies had finally fessed up that they had killed him. The three of them got into a drunken fight that day and tried to kill each other. One of 'em did.

Anyway, he knew somehow I was back in Clement and came to see me several times. It took him almost six months to convince me to come back and take over his job. He didn't give up easy."

He was rambling.

"Zak."

"Kizzie, I would give anything to take back that day. I keep seeing Miss Lizzie. She was so scared of that river anyway. She must have been terrified. I've asked myself a million times what would have happened if I hadn't gone back to get my stuff. If I had tied the second anchor before I left…"

She interrupted with kisses all over his face, his ears, his neck. Then she sat back down.

"Zak, it wouldn't have made a difference. It wasn't your fault. The winds were too strong that day. There was nothing you or anyone else could've done. The wind had pushed them too far from the dock. You have to believe that Zak. If I had stopped caring about Kizzie long enough to accept that, I wouldn't have lost so much time away from my family and this wonderful town. I wouldn't have been the cause of so much pain for Seal. Or you Zak. Zak, it was just their time to go. And they went the way they would have wanted. They died together. She came around to face him. She sank to her knees.

"I love you Clifford Zacharias Bishop. I am so sorry it took me so long to get around to telling you that. I love you with all my heart, deep inside my soul I love you. I'm so sorry for everything Zak...for not trusting you, for taking your love for granted all these years, for not being here when you needed me. Would you forgive me? Please forgive me Zak? And if you let me, I promise I'll spend the rest of my life making it up to you."

Zak took a few minutes to think about what she said. It was time to let it all go. If there was something to be punished for, they had all suffered the price.

Zak could only stand to see her suffer for a few minutes at a time.

"Hmmm, sounds to me like you might be trying to open up negotiations..."

He pulled her up to straddle his lap. His arms went around her in a perfect fit. She pressed her head into the cusp of his neck between his chin and his shoulder. The beat of his heart matched the rhythm of her own. Have your own way Love was the tune she thought she heard.

She whispered softly."Let the bargaining begin."

"Hey."
"Hey."
"Hey Kizzie?"
"Hey Zak?'
"Will you marry me."
"Just try and stop me."

About the Author

Bre Smith was the eleventh of thirteen siblings born to sharecropper parents. Hers was not unlike any number of other working class families of the 1950s. Absent the presence of TV, daily newspapers or even a local library, the large family of natural storytellers relied on their wit, humor and imagination as their greatest source of entertainment. As a child Bre admired the free-flow, uncomplicated way they could weave ordinary life events into wonderful stories. But it would be years later that she would come to recognize the value of those family gatherings on the front porch and to appreciate the impact those early memories had on her love of reading and the written word.

Her appreciation for the power of words grew, along with her talent for writing, during the twenty years she spent in various assignments in the communications industry. With self determination, the guidance of caring mentors and God's blessings, she used her creative talent to develop a successful career writing for corporate business executives.

In 2007 Bre had reached a crossroad. The stress of ever changing uncertainties in the business environment and great personal challenges weighed heavily on her emotional and physical well being. Looking for self inspiration and motivation she took the advice of friends and associates who encouraged her to put her talent to work to weave her own story. Let Love Have Its Way is the result of her commitment to rejuvenate her life and in the process, realize her dream to become an author. This is her first published work.

Bre lives and works in Jacksonville, Florida.

Printed in the United States
135097LV00001B/2/P

9 781438 919379